You're invited to a

CREEPOVER

Together Forever

written by P. J. Night

SIMON SPOTLIGHT
New York   London   Toronto   Sydney   New Delhi

This book is a work of fiction. Any references to historical events, real people, or real locales are used fictitiously. Other names, characters, places, and incidents are the product of the author's imagination, and any resemblance to actual events or locales or persons, living or dead, is entirely coincidental.

SIMON SPOTLIGHT
An imprint of Simon & Schuster Children's Publishing Division
1230 Avenue of the Americas, New York, New York 10020
Copyright © 2012 by Simon & Schuster, Inc.
All rights reserved, including the right of reproduction in whole or in part in any form.
SIMON SPOTLIGHT and colophon are registered trademarks of Simon & Schuster, Inc.
YOU'RE INVITED TO A CREEPOVER is a trademark of Simon & Schuster, Inc.
Text by Lara Bergen
For information about special discounts for bulk purchases, please contact Simon & Schuster Special Sales at 1-866-506-1949 or business@simonandschuster.com.
Manufactured in the United States of America 0413 OFF
First Edition 10 9 8 7 6 5 4 3
ISBN 978-1-4424-5159-9
ISBN 978-1-4424-5160-5 (eBook)
Library of Congress Catalog Card Number 2012933332

CHAPTER 1

"Who-*whoo*! Who-*whooo*!"

Jennifer Howard looked up. Was that an *owl*? How could it be that late already?

She kept moving, but she could feel a nervous knot growing tighter in her throat. She knew she shouldn't be out in the woods so late, all alone.

And yet she couldn't turn back. It was as if something were leading her—pulling her even—steadily down the trail, the very same one she'd hiked with her five bunkmates earlier that day. Yes, there was the fallen tree on which Sam had somehow done a whole balance beam routine. And there was the amazing giant mushroom that her twin sister, Ali, had kicked. It lay there now, bruised and broken, and for an instant made Jennifer annoyed at her bunkmate all over again.

And then suddenly she noticed something she hadn't seen before. Right there, where the trail veered right at the stone marker, overgrown with ferns and other twisting, gnarled weeds, another path went straight. It was much narrower than the Old Stump Trail, but there was no doubt it was a path . . . and Jennifer's feet, at least, thought it was the path she ought to take.

But where did it lead? The brush was so wild and dense that Jennifer could barely see where it was safe to step. Plus whatever light was left in the sky was quickly draining away. There was nothing ahead of her but eerie, ominous shadows—and soon behind her as well. She pulled out her compass to try to get her bearings. Her hands were trembling and she fought against her nerves to keep them still. She waited for the needle to steady and find its way north. It finally stopped, and she discovered north was exactly the way that the trail led.

Hey, she thought, her mood suddenly brightening. Directly north was Camp Hiawatha, their brother camp across the lake! What if the trail was a shortcut to the boys' camp? That would be the find of the century. Wait till she told the other girls! Now she *had* to keep going, she told herself, if only to see if the trail took her there.

She picked up her pace and pushed through the branches, trying not to get too tangled or scratched in the jutting roots or dead tree limbs. At last she burst out of the woods and into a clearing. She stopped at once and looked around.

The clearing, she could see, was about the size of a softball diamond and bathed in a misty, greenish light. The only structure was a lonely-looking, small log cabin that had to have been a hundred years old. Jennifer briefly wondered about the person who built it and why. The door dangled, cockeyed, from its hinges beneath a roof that looked ready to fall in. Of the two windows that she could see, one was broken and one was roughly boarded up. Clearly, nobody had occupied this cabin for a very long time.

And yet it somehow didn't seem empty.

Jennifer took a half step toward the cabin.

Then paused. Something didn't feel right.

Her blood felt cold all of a sudden, as if her heart had turned to ice. *I shouldn't go any farther,* she told herself, backing up, and before she knew it she was running away. But wait! She slid to a halt and her head whipped around in search of the path. All she could see was a solid black wall of trees.

The trail had disappeared.

Plus it was fully night now, she realized. Way too dark to see into the woods. The clearing was somehow still glowing, but all around it there was nothing but shadows and the dark spaces between the trees. Jennifer could only imagine what was in there, watching her. One step in the wrong direction could mean getting lost, or injured, or worse. And who knew how long it would be until someone found her. It could be too late by the time they did.

Okay. No problem, Jennifer thought, holding up her compass and trying her best to keep her head. *South.* That was all she needed to know. But when she looked down, the needle was spinning. She guessed it was just her trembling hands. But no. Her hands weren't shaking any worse than before. In fact they were still, she realized. The needle was spinning all by itself.

Anxious, she tapped the side of the compass, but that didn't seem to help. She gave it a shake and willed it to *stop* already and do what it needed to do. But the harder she stared at the needle, the faster and faster it turned. Jennifer listened and could even hear it making a tiny, frantic *whirr*.

Now her hands were trembling. Her whole body was, in fact.

"Who-*whoo*."

Startled, she jumped. Then she closed her eyes and caught her breath. It was the owl from the trail.

"*Whooo*."

Or was it?

She slowly turned back toward the cabin, not sure if her ears were playing tricks. Could it be that the call was coming from *it*?

"He-hello?" she softly called. She took another step into the clearing, and this time she didn't stop. There wasn't just something in the cabin. There was *someone*. Maybe that someone could help her find her way back to camp!

"Hello?" she called again as she reached the door. She listened, but there was no answer. She waited and almost knocked. But then she noticed the broken window there right beside her. What if she simply peeked in? She leaned over. What remained of the glass was too caked with dirt and grime to actually see through. But the jagged hole would work, she guessed. She leaned in closer and peered through.

Was it?

Yes, it was!

There was a person sitting in there with his back to her and a hooded sweatshirt pulled down low over his head. It was a boy. At least she thought so, but she wasn't completely sure. . . .

That is until he pulled the sweatshirt back and slowly turned.

His face was pale and boyishly handsome, but it was his eyes—or lack of them, really—that Jennifer saw first. Where his eyes should have been, there were laserlike beams of greenish light. They shot straight toward her, and she shrank back. She tried to scream, but nothing came out. Her blood, her lungs, her whole body felt numb.

Run! she tried to tell herself.

But she was too terrified to move.

Finally she managed to scramble away from the window, not knowing or caring which way she went. It didn't matter to her anymore what might be lurking out in the dark woods. She needed to get out of that clearing, she knew, as fast as she possibly could. But she'd barely run ten yards when she felt a sharp tug on the back of her shirt.

She stumbled back, afraid to turn, but she could feel a laserlike burn on the back of her head.

"Don't ever come back," said a low, haunting voice in her ear.

And that's when the scream finally spilled out of her throat.

CHAPTER 2

"Ayghyhhh!!"

Jennifer Howard woke up in a cold sweat and frantically looked around. It took a good minute for her heart to stop racing and for her eyes to assure her that, yes, she was fine and perfectly safe in her cozy wooden cot in Bunk 9.

"Are you okay?" Megan Daugherty called down from the bunk above. She leaned over the side, and her long hair dangled like a blond curtain near Jennifer's face.

"Don't tell me you had a nightmare too!" said Georgia Mallory, hopping out of her own bunk and plopping down on Jennifer's cot, right on her legs.

"Ow! Did I ever!" Jennifer answered. "I'm sorry if I woke you guys up. It was just so scary—and it seemed so *real!*" She covered her face with her hot-pink polka-dotted sheet. "I don't even want to talk about it!"

"Let me guess," said Georgia. "It all started with you hiking, all la-di-da, down the Old Stump Trail. And then you came to this *other* little overgrown trail and took it."

"Yeah." Jennifer lowered her covers a few inches to just below her nose. "How did you know?" she asked.

"Then did you come to this creepy clearing?" said Megan.

"And was there a cabin?" Stefi Simon added. She was up in the bunk above Georgia's with Bingo, her floppy stuffed black-and-white puppy, held tightly to her chest. "And a super, I mean *super*, creepy dude inside—with these freaky glowing eyes?"

Jennifer stared at them all, her mouth open. "I don't get it! How do you know what I dreamed? Was I talking in my sleep?"

Georgia grinned and shook her head, which was covered in thick dark curls. "Unh-unh. You're not going to believe this, but we all had the same nightmare! *Exactly!*" she said.

Jennifer gasped. "No way . . ." She looked from

Georgia to Megan to Stefi. They pretended to shiver and nodded back.

Stefi crossed her heart and Bingo's. "Yep. We totally did. We swear."

"Wow." It took a few seconds for the crazy idea to sink in. "What do you think it *means*?" Jennifer asked at last.

Megan shrugged along with Stefi. "I don't know. Did he tell you, 'Don't ever come back'? As far as I'm concerned, that works for me!" she said.

"No problemo!" said Jennifer, nodding. "I don't care how many demerits Gwen gives us. I'm never hiking around there again!"

"Well, luckily, I don't think we have to worry since we go home in a few days anyway," Georgia said. "Hey, maybe it's some kind of supernatural 'so long' joke from good old Minnehaha. What do you think?"

"I think if it is, she has a *terrible* sense of humor!" Jennifer said.

"Aghhhh! Let me go!"

"Hey, it's Ali!" Stefi exclaimed, waving Bingo.

The girls all turned to the farthest bunk, where Ali Harmon, a redheaded girl in green striped pajamas was fitfully rocking from side to side.

"Should I go wake her up?" Jennifer asked.

"Oh, I don't know," Georgia replied, wincing.

"Yeah." Stefi nodded. "You know how much she hates that."

Jennifer nodded. By now they all knew—all too well. Getting Ali up in the morning was like getting a chicken to lay an egg. She got up when she was good and ready, no matter how many hands-on-hips or demerits she got from their counselor, Gwen.

"But look at her," said Jennifer. Ali was thrashing now and yelling something they couldn't quite make out. "I have to," she said as she hopped out of bed.

"Good luck!" Megan called down.

Jennifer reached Ali and shook her shoulder. "Ali! Wake up! It's okay! You were just having a nightmare. You're perfectly safe."

Ali whimpered and stopped tossing, but her eyes stayed tightly shut.

"It was just a dream," Jennifer went on. "Don't worry, Ali. You're fine. Were you in the woods, and was a boy chasing you? Did he live in an old cabin and have glowing eyes? If that was your dream, then guess what? We *all* had the same nightmare last night!"

11

"Huh?" Ali finally squinted up at her, though she still looked ninety-nine percent asleep. "What time is it?" she muttered groggily.

"I don't know," Jennifer said. There was no clock or TV or anything else in their cabin that might tell them the time. Even their cell phones were off and wedged deep in their trunks. It was one of many Camp Minnehaha rules. Jennifer guessed. "Maybe seven o'clock?"

"*Ugh.*" Ali yanked her covers up over her chin and flipped onto her side. "Then I'm going back to sleep. We don't even have to be up yet. Why'd you have to wake me?"

"You're going back to sleep?" Megan slid down off her bunk now. "Ali! How can you even close your eyes? Aren't you afraid that awful dream might come back?" she asked.

"No," Ali groaned. It was one dumb dream. She'd seen scary movies and read scary stories that were a whole lot worse.

"And you don't think it's weird that we all had the same one?" Stefi went on.

Ali eyed her over her shoulder. "No. Actually, what I

think is *weird* is that you still sleep with a doll."

"It's a *dog*," Stefi quietly corrected her. "And his name is Bingo." She kissed his head.

"Oh, let her go back to sleep," said Georgia with a weary wave of her hand. After four weeks in the same cabin at Camp Minnehaha, they were all used to Ali's moods and tried to avoid them as best they could. Mornings were the worst, but some afternoons and evenings were just as bad. Honestly, they didn't know how Ali's twin sister, Sam, could stand living with her year-round.

"Hey, so did Sam have the same dream too?" Jennifer asked Georgia. She scratched a bugbite on her knee.

"I don't know," Georgia replied. She pointed to the neatly made bunk above Ali's. "As usual, she was already gone by the time I got up."

That was something else Bunk 9 was used to: Sam's waking up with the sun. She was always up and out of the cabin long before anyone else. If she wasn't raising the flag, she was there to salute it first thing. Then sometimes she'd do yoga with the counselors, or help with breakfast in the mess hall. And she didn't stop there. She kept going all day. None of them had ever known someone so full of energy and eager to try anything and everything.

"You didn't hear Sam cry out or anything, did you, Ali?" Megan asked.

"Earth to Megan, can't you see I'm *sleeping*?" Ali grumbled. "Or at least I *was*. Will you please leave me alone?"

"Whatever," huffed Megan. "Come on, guys, let's get dressed and go eat."

"Sounds good. Hey, has anyone seen my toothbrush?" Georgia asked as she grabbed her plastic bathroom tote.

Ali lay there with her eyes clamped shut, tired, but still tense from her dream. And though she never would admit it to the other girls in her cabin, she actually was curious about what a shared nightmare might mean. Four weeks ago, in fact, it might have actually gotten her out of her bunk and sent her off to join the other girls. And there was a part of her still that wanted to—it just wasn't strong enough. It was too late for that, she'd decided. And besides, the girls weren't *her* friends; they were her sister Sam's friends. Ali had given up on making friends at camp, just like she'd given up back at school. That was the thing about being Sam Harmon's sister:

There was simply no way on earth to compete with her. Nothing Ali said or did mattered, it seemed, when Sam was around. She got all the attention all the time, and Ali was used to it by now. She couldn't remember a time, in fact, when Sam didn't outshine her and make her feel small. There was only one way in which Ali stood out, and that was the birthmark on the side of her chin. It was like a sign that said SAM'S PERFECT, BUT POOR ALI'S A BIG MESS. Sure, people said they didn't even notice it, but how could they not? Especially at camp, where they were always doing something active and she had to throw her hair up into a ponytail every day. The mark was the size and shape of a prune and the color of a bruise dipped in blood. It was all Ali saw when she looked in the mirror, and all she didn't see when she looked at Sam. And she was sure it gave all the girls in the camp plenty to laugh about behind her back.

CHAPTER 3

By the time Ali got to the mess hall that morning, most of the camp had been there for a while. The long tables were just starting to empty, but the smell of bacon was still strong. This was where the girls ate all their meals, unless they had a cookout by the campfire or took their lunch on a hike. It wasn't too different from Ali's school cafeteria, except that everything—the tables and chairs, the floor, the walls—was made of wood. And just like her school cafeteria, it was a chamber of torture for her.

Ali quickly scanned Bunk 9's benches but saw right away that Sam wasn't there. She'd probably already eaten, Ali figured, and was back in the kitchen working hard to earn extra brownie points. She thought about sitting down with her bunkmates at their table—but just for a second, then she changed her mind. It was a lot easier to skip breakfast or just eat some cereal standing up than to sit there knowing everyone wished that she weren't there. Besides, she wasn't that hungry, and she almost turned to leave. Then she heard a "Yoo-hoo! Sleepyhead!" behind her. She turned and saw Sam waving through the wide window between the camp kitchen and the dining room.

"I've been waiting for you!" Sam called to her. "Come here. Hurry up."

Ali sighed and crossed the mess hall and went through the wide swinging door that divided the two rooms. Sam was standing by the deep stainless steel sink, in which a huge stack of dirty dishes was precariously piled.

"Guess what?" Sam said, smiling brightly.

"Ah, the other Harmon twin. Hello Ali," greeted Kay, the camp cook. Ali chose to ignore her and turned to Sam.

"Kay and I made blueberry muffins this morning, and you almost missed them. You're lucky I saved you one. Here." She wiped her hands on a towel and pulled a muffin carefully wrapped in a napkin down off a shelf.

Ali took it and unwrapped it. The muffin was still warm. "Thanks," she murmured, already weary of the

17

word she'd probably be telling Sam all day.

"Oh, don't thank me. Thank Kay!" Sam said. She turned to the short, suntanned woman who was scraping the grill. A faded red bandana held back her graying hair. "These are so good, Kay! Next summer, can you make them every day? *Please?*" Sam begged.

"For you, I wish, Sam," Kay told her. "But where am I going to get all those blueberries? They don't grow on trees, you know," she joked.

Sam slipped her arm through Ali's elbow. "Ali and I could pick them for you! Couldn't we, Ali?" she said.

"Uh . . ." Ali shrugged and took a big bite of muffin, since picking berries in the buggy woods was about the last thing she wanted to do. Then she jumped and looked down, surprised to feel something soft and warm wind around her leg.

It was the cook's glossy black cat, Magic. "Hey there." Ali reached down and rubbed her hand along his soft back.

Kay smiled as he arched it appreciatively. "He likes you, Ali," she said. "I can hear him purring from all the way over here."

At least someone here likes me, thought Ali, though she couldn't help but grin. Then Sam bent down and

18

scooped him out from under Ali's hand.

"Oh, who's a cutie?" she cooed, rubbing noses with him. "You like me, too, don't you, Magic? Yes, you do!"

Ali looked down at the half muffin she still had left and tossed it into the big black trash can.

"Hey, can I get you anything else, Ali?" Kay asked her. "Grill's still hot. How 'bout some eggs?"

"No." Ali shook her head hard from side to side. "I hate eggs," she declared.

"Okay, well, if you want anything else, just let me know. You'll probably be glad to get back to home cooking, won't you?"

"Yeah." Ali nodded. "I guess."

"Well, just two more days!" Kay reminded her warmly.

"Aw, don't remind me!" Sam pouted, raising her head from Magic's ears. "I already can't wait for *next* summer. I'm going to miss it here so much!"

Ali rolled her eyes. *Of course Sam is going to miss camp,* she thought. From archery to zip-lining, she'd won certificates in everything. Plus all the counselors adored her, and she'd made a million friends. Ali, on the other hand, had made exactly none. And the really sad thing was that she'd actually tried this time. In the beginning, at least. Kind of.

Who knew? Maybe if she and Sam been in different cabins she might have made her own friends. But with Sam around, it was hopeless. She always felt like some kind of big, flat fifth wheel. Plus sleeping in a bunk in a cabin in the middle of nowhere just wasn't Ali's idea of fun at all.

But Kay was right. It was almost over. Just two more days, then she'd be home. And what was the first thing Ali was telling her parents when they came to pick her up? That she was never coming back to Camp Minneha-ha ever again! Of course, she knew they'd just find some-where else to ship her off to next summer. They couldn't wait to send her away. But whatever, that was fine. Just so it wasn't back here with Sam and a bunch of girls who didn't get her and never would. And maybe it would be good to get out from under Sam's shadow at long last—though Sam's shadow was huge. Ali always dreamed of their trading places, but that was a dream that never came true. Perhaps if they were apart, at least, she could have her own life and discover who she really was.

"How 'bout you, Ali? You gonna miss it here?" The cook eyed her, and Ali replied with a half-hearted shrug.

Sam squeezed her sister's arm. "Oh, *Ali!* Don't mind

her, Kay. My sister's a girl of few words. Hey, thanks for letting me help. We'd better be off to pottery now. They were supposed to fire our pieces last night, and I can't wait to see how the glaze on my fruit bowl turned out."

"See you girls later," the cook replied, shaking her head as the twins walked off. *Boy, those girls couldn't look more alike—or be more different,* she thought.

"So!" Sam said as soon as they got outside. "How did *you* sleep last night?"

Ali groaned, remembering the nightmare that she'd *almost* erased from her brain. "Terribly," she told Sam. "Thanks a lot for reminding me. Why?" She suddenly turned to her sister. "Hey, did *you* have a crazy dream last night too?"

Sam stopped in her tracks and nodded. "I did!" She smiled.

"Wow . . . weird," said Ali slowly.

"Weird *awesome!*" Sam gushed.

"*Awesome?*" Ali's nose wrinkled. She didn't understand. "What do you mean by 'awesome'? *Scary* awesome?" she asked.

Sam looked at her a little cockeyed. "No, awesome as in *wonderful!*" she said. "I mean, yeah, maybe it was a little scary at first, when I was walking through the woods." Then she chewed her lip and considered it. "No. You know, actually, even that part was pretty great too. Want me to describe it?"

Ali opened her mouth to speak, but Sam kept going.

"I remember it perfectly!" Sam took a deep breath and rubbed her hands. "It was kind of late, almost twilight, and I was hiking down that Old Stump Trail—you know, the one our bunk hiked yesterday—but I was hiking it all alone. The woods were really peaceful and the birds were singing and the sun was shining down through all the trees. It was just like the woods in a princess movie. Seriously! And then I suddenly found this *other* trail by accident. But it wasn't an accident either, I guess, because it was like it was put there for me to find. So of course I took it, and I followed it for a while, and then I came to this really beautiful clearing full of flowers, and there was this cute little cabin."

Ali's lip had been slowly curling. "Cute?" she managed to get in at last.

Sam nodded. "Adorable! But not half as cute as what I found inside." She wiggled her eyebrows and grinned.

Ali frowned. "A boy," she said.

"Yes! How'd you guess?" said Sam. "I went up to the window and peeked in—the cabin was so sweet, I just had to, you know—and there he was, sitting there, this cute boy, and when he saw me looking in, he smiled the cutest, sweetest smile—and his *eyes*, they were practically silver, and *magnetic*, I swear."

"Magnetic." Ali's nerves began to tense as she tried to make sense of what she was hearing. So her sister had *basically* had the same dream as everyone else, but instead of being superscary, hers had been supergreat.

Sam, meanwhile, giggled. "Ali, why are you repeating everything I say?"

Ali clenched her jaw and ignored her. "Okay, so this 'cute boy.' Did he chase you? Or anything?" she asked.

Sam shook her head dreamily. "I wish!" she laughed. "In *fact*," she went on, "I've been thinking ever since I woke up that I should try to find that trail this afternoon. I mean, what if the dream's a premonition and he really is there? I could use our free time after swimming." She noticed Ali's expression and sighed. "Okay, I know I'm crazy. But honestly, Ali, the dream felt so real! I can't think about anything else. You know how that is. I feel as if I *have* to try to find it. What do you think?"

She looked at her twin with wide, hopeful eyes. "Well? Anything? Hmm? Say something, please!"

But Ali said nothing. She couldn't even begin to tell Sam what she was thinking, which was basically *No way, not again.* Leave it to her sister to have a *sweet* dream when everyone else in the cabin had a nightmare. So great a dream, in fact, that it was tempting Miss Goody Two-shoes to go off hiking by herself, which they both knew very well meant breaking one of Camp Minnehaha's top-five do-not-break rules.

Yes, Ali knew all too well what it was like to think about one thing and nothing else. She was actually thinking about one thing right then, in fact: how her twin sister's life was charmed, and hers was cursed.

Sam wrung her hands. "Oh, I know. You don't have to say it, Ali. I'm getting carried away. I think if you'd had this same dream, though, you'd kind of understand. Hey, what made you think to ask me about my dream anyway? Did you have a vivid dream last night too?"

Ali stared straight ahead, toward the arts-and-crafts hut coming up on their right. "Nope. Nothing. No dream," she muttered. "And, for the record, I think believing in dreams is just plain dumb."

CHAPTER 4

"I'm going to do it."

Ali groaned as her sister caught up to her on the path back from the lake. They'd just finished swimming, their last "official" activity of the day. The girls were in different groups, however, since Sam could do all the strokes *and* dive. Ali, on the other hand, had pretty much decided on the first day of camp not to bother even trying.

They now had a few hours of free time before dinner, and the sun was still bright overhead. Clusters of girls trotted past them, wrapped in bright towels and chatting happily away.

"Hi, Sam! Congrats on passing the lifesaving test today!" a bunch of them called.

"Thanks! Thanks a lot!" Sam grinned and waved back to them, while Ali kept her eyes down and trudged on ahead.

"What are you going to do?" she asked Sam finally. "Swim the English Channel now that you've passed every other test?"

"Uh, no," Sam replied patiently. She was used to her sister's sarcasm. Still, sometimes she wished she'd give it a break. Just like she wished Ali didn't always try to make her feel bad for simply trying to do her very best.

She draped her damp towel around her shoulders, where it caught the cool lake water dripping from her hair. "I'm going to go look for that trail," Sam said. "The one I saw in my dream. I just decided we're only here two more days and we have this free time today, and, well, I might not get another chance to get away—so why not?"

Ali turned to her with raised eyebrows. "And what if Gwen finds out?" she asked.

Sam sighed at the mention of their cabin counselor, who'd told them specifically not to ever go hiking alone. She actually couldn't believe she was even considering breaking such a basic rule. Her stomach clenched in a tight knot at the thought of Gwen finding out. But at the same time, all the rest of her was urging her to go.

Half smiling and half wincing, Sam knit her fingers together and held them just below her chin. "That's kind of why I'm telling you, Ali. I was hoping you could cover for me? *Please?*" she begged.

Ali grinned. *This is interesting,* she thought.

She slowly raised her own chin so that she was looking down her nose. It wasn't often Sam asked *her* for favors, and she couldn't help enjoying the feeling—a lot. Usually she was asking Sam to cover for *her*. It seemed Ali was always being grounded, or at least on the verge. In fact, she was currently "on probation" at camp for skipping her animal care chores four or five too many times. (And it would have been a lot more if Sam hadn't gone ahead and done them in her place.) But really, could Ali help it if the smell of the chicken coop made her sick? It wouldn't help the chickens much to throw up all over them.

"I mean, I don't want to get you in trouble," Sam added quickly. "And if you don't feel right, I understand. But if she asks you where I am, and you don't mind *too* much . . ."

Ali laid her hands on Sam's damp shoulders. "Of course I'll do it," she assured her sister. "After all the times you've helped me out. And you know me,"—she grinned—"I'm pretty good at making things up."

Sam nodded. It was true. Few things came to her sister quite as easily as telling lies. "Thanks, Ali." She sighed. "Really, you're the best! And don't worry," she said. "I'll bet Gwen doesn't even ask about me."

"Yeah, probably not," Ali agreed. "It's not like you're her favorite camper or anything." She watched Sam's eyes dim with worry, and she gave her arm a pat. "I'm just kidding, of course. Don't sweat it. I bet she'll be way too busy getting ready for the dance at the boys' camp tonight."

"The dance!" cried Sam. "Oh, that's right. I'll have to hurry back. Do you know, I've been thinking about this *dream* so much, I almost forgot about it."

"Really?" Ali frowned and wanted to kick herself right then for even bringing the subject up. *How great would it be,* she suddenly thought, *if Sam didn't go.* The dance was the "big event" of the end of their four weeks and was being held at the boys' camp. But if it was anything like their school dances, Ali knew exactly how it would be. All the boys would flock around Sam like pigeons around a big bag of birdseed. And whom would they completely ignore? Her. Ali.

"Well, hurry back so you can get ready!" Ali said, smiling the sweetest smile she could. Only she knew that she didn't mean a single word.

Sam left Ali and hurried back to Bunk 9. She wanted to change out of her swimsuit and head off into the woods before any of her bunkmates returned. She didn't want to have to explain where she was going, or why she didn't want to hang out and spend the rest of the day getting ready for the dance. She wasn't a very good liar for one thing (despite the fact that she won *I Doubt It* almost every time they played), and she wasn't sure how they'd take the truth if she told them. Ali, she could tell anything. Sam didn't have to worry about what she thought. But she had a certain image to maintain around the rest of the world. She could just hear herself saying, *I'm going to go chase some cute boy from a crazy dream I had last night.* Yeah, right. They'd either think she was insane, or they'd want to go along. And if they went and they didn't find anything, she'd feel like a total idiot.

Dressed in long jeans (in order to be extra safe traipsing through the woods) and a plain white T-shirt, she soon headed back outside. She quickly cut through the volleyball court and the campfire circle until she reached the head of the Old Stump Trail. The sun shone brightly where she stood, and she paused as she gazed down the mossy path. It curved almost immediately, disappearing into the dark woods. Was she really about to hike down it right now all by herself? It was *so* unlike her to go and break a rule. Plus there were reasons why campers weren't allowed to go off in the woods by themselves. Good ones, she knew. But she'd be fine, she told herself. She'd be very, *very* careful. After all, she was probably the most careful and most accomplished hiker in the whole camp.

She set off, at once enjoying the peace and shade of the gentle trail. After four weeks at camp, she'd come to think of the tall oaks and pines all around her as old, faithful friends. From their graceful braches high above, songbirds called back and forth, and off somewhere in the distance Sam could hear a woodpecker hammering steadily, hard at work. This wasn't a nature walk though, she knew. She didn't have all day. She focused on finding a second trail—the one she'd dreamed of—and picked up her pace.

Before long she came to the spot where the trail was blocked by an old fallen tree. She remembered finding it the day before and how she'd stopped and done the little balance beam routine. It was a bit show-offy, she knew, but she loved gymnastics so much. And everyone seemed to appreciate her perfect walkover and clean round-off. This time, though, she simply hopped over the trunk and continued on her way. She had to be getting close. *Yes!* There was the trail marker pointing right. In her dream she was almost positive that the other trail started just about there. But as she took a few more steps she began to doubt herself.

Was it just a silly dream after all? she thought. She was beginning to be very glad that she didn't gush about it to anyone but her sister.

But wait! She hurried forward. There was a trail. *Maybe it is real!* she told herself.

Sure enough, where the main trail bent right, a much narrower trail went straight. It was overgrown and, if a person wasn't looking for it, extremely easy to miss. But it was just like in her dream—right down to the tangle of spidery ferns reaching all the way up to her knees. She picked up her feet and carefully stepped through them. She stayed on her toes. *Please don't let there be any snakes!* she thought. The needle-like briars were bad enough anyway. They stretched from spindly brambles on either side. They grabbed like hooks on to her hair and her clothes, as well as the bare skin on her arms. She kept one hand in front of her eyes, worried that any minute a rogue thorn might poke one out.

"*Ouch!*" she cried as a thin branch she'd pushed aside whipped back, straight into her chin. Determined, though, she kept going, ducking and dodging as best she could. She hadn't remembered this part of the trail being quite so excruciating in her dream the night before.

She tried to peer ahead through the tangle of limbs for a clearing, but it was no use. All she could see were more and more branches—and less and less trail. For a moment she actually froze, afraid that she might have lost her way. But no sooner had she stopped than her feet began to move again. Her mind had no idea where she was going, but her body didn't seem to care. She felt like a leaf in a river being carried steadily out to sea by the current. She had no intention of turning back, but somehow she knew it would have been hard—impossible even—if she tried.

And then at last she glimpsed a golden ray of warm light that lit her up inside, as well. The next thing she knew, the ferns and branches gave way and she was no longer in the woods. Instead she was at the edge of a sunny clearing on a lush carpet of emerald grass. Here and there the deep green was dotted with clusters of delicate blue flowers. The flowers were so blue, they seemed to glow. Dainty white butterflies flitted between them like sociable fairies with jobs to do. A scent like nothing she'd ever smelled before filled her nose. She took a deep breath and held it for a moment, then let out a soft contented sigh.

And there it was. The cozy cabin. It was just like in her dream! Sam felt like a little girl on Christmas morning who had just opened the greatest gift in the whole world. There was only one question now: Was there also a boy inside waiting for her?

What was *she* waiting for? Sam took off toward the cabin in a jog that soon turned into a full-out run. There was a thick patch of dry leaves between her and the cabin, but it never occurred to her to go around it, or even to clear it with a jump. Instead she charged straight through, and almost immediately she felt the spongy ground fall out from under her.

Instinctively Sam screamed as she plummeted straight down. She landed at last with a thud, on her back on a floor that was made of cold, hard dirt. She lay there in shock, unable to move or breathe. The wind had been completely knocked out of her. She couldn't see either, she realized. Her eyes were open, but it was black. For a moment, all she could think was, *Am I dead?*

Then at last her lungs recovered. Desperately she gasped for air. Gradually, too, her eyes adjusted to the darkness of the hole. She wiggled her toes and fingers and gently turned her head. Nothing was broken. That was good, at least. But the place she was in was bad. Really bad.

It was a deep, dank pit that she realized wasn't that much bigger than her cot back at Bunk 9. She barely had to move her hands to feel the damp walls of earth all around. She sensed a small tickle on the back of her hand and thought she could make out a gleaming black shell. It was some sort of beetle. *Ew!* She cringed and flicked it off, but it didn't go far. Then something else slipped behind her ear—she could feel it crawling. It moved into her hair. She let out a whimper and frantically swiped at her head.

Miles above her, it seemed, a patch of dull sky shone through a web of roots and heavy leaves. She crawled to her knees, but she knew before she even stood up how hard climbing out of the hole would be. She felt all around, but there was nothing to grab and nowhere to brace her feet. She rose to her toes, stretched her arms up as high as she possibly could, and jumped. But no, the top edge of the hole was *still* out of reach. *If I were only a little taller!* she thought.

"*Help!*"

The word spilled out of her mouth in a single, desperate cry. She knew no one back at camp could ever hear her. She was much too far away. But maybe, just maybe, the boy from her dream was out there somewhere, and maybe he would hear her scream.

"*Help!*" she yelled again, this time even louder. "*I'm down here!*" she called. "*I'm in a hole!*"

Then she waited and tried to listen for a sound other than her thundering heart.

There was nothing at first. Only silence—as if the whole world had paused.

And then, like a summer shower, it started. One grain of dirt, and then another, and another, and another began to rain down.

Sam began to say hello, but before she could finish, she caught the word and sucked it back.

There was something up there, but the way it was pawing and scraping made her stomach suddenly twist in fear. Who could it be? What if it wasn't even human, let alone the boy of her dreams? A boy, after all, would say something—like "Hang on! I'm coming!"—wouldn't he? A boy wouldn't be tearing away at the earth like a ravenous wild animal stalking helpless prey.

And there she was, like a fly in a web. Whatever was up there would get her. There was no way to escape.

CHAPTER 5

Sam squatted down and squeezed her eyes shut tight and covered her face with her trembling hands. Dirt was pouring down now in thick, gritty clumps, and suddenly she felt a whole new fear along with it.

I'm going to be buried alive! she thought hysterically.

Which was worse? Being eaten by some kind of wild animal? Or being swallowed by the earth?

Either thought made her eyes well up and overflow with salty tears.

She had to get out of the pit, and yet how could she? She was trapped.

But maybe, she told herself, *just maybe, if I'm still and very quiet, whatever's up there will go away.*

She crouched down as low as she possibly could and

curled herself into a tight ball. She tried her best not to breathe or make the slightest movement or noise. But she couldn't make herself stop shivering—either from fear, or cold, or both.

I never should have gone off by myself! she thought. *What was I thinking, breaking the rules? If I get out of this, I'll never, ever break another one!*

Then gradually she realized something. The soil had stopped falling on her back. She listened. The pit was silent. There was no more scratching noise from up above.

Sam lifted her head slowly and ever so cautiously opened her eyes. Once again she looked up to see, high above, a shaft of pale light. She pulled herself to her feet, still shaking, and brushed the dirt out of her hair. She let out the breath that she'd been holding and replaced it with a gulp of cold, dank air.

It's gone! she thought. *Oh, please, please let it be true.*

She listened again. There was nothing. *It's going to be okay,* she told herself.

She was suddenly weak with relief. She still had to get out of the hole, of course, but she knew if she tried, she could figure it out. She just had to stay calm and try not to let her imagination get so carried away this time. She took a deep breath and lifted her arms up in preparation to jump. She *would* get out of this hole.

Then she blinked as a single grain of dirt dropped down onto her upturned cheek.

It's just dirt, she told herself. *No reason to freak out.*

The reason came soon enough, though, when a clawlike hand plunged down in one swift motion through the earth. The fingers were spread wide open and headed straight for Sam. She screamed and tried to jerk away from it, but the hole was just too small. The hand found her in an instant and grabbed for her, as if it had eyes of its own. The dirt-caked digits clamped down around Sam's raised hand, and in one swift, heart-stopping motion, they snatched her up, past the rim of crushed, bruised leaves, and out onto the ragged edge of the hole.

"No!!!"

"It's okay. It's okay. I didn't mean to hurt you." Sam heard a soft and soothing voice. It was hard to make out what was being said, though, between Sam's piercing screams.

She was bent over her knees, quaking, frantically clutching her tender fingers. She could hear the person speaking to her, but she couldn't look up yet. Instead she looked down at two well-worn sneakers attached to two long, denim-covered legs.

"Are you okay? I'm glad I was able to get you out of there," someone went on.

Slowly Sam's eyes traveled up, past a thick red hooded sweatshirt, and into the smiling eyes of a boy her age.

Her shivering stopped and her mouth fell open. "It's *you!*" she gasped, rearing back on her heels and nearly tumbling back into the hole.

Swiftly the boy moved to catch her, reaching out to take both her hands. This time his hands felt gentle, and a sharp tingle surged straight through Sam's body, like a mild electric shock. She bit her lip and wondered if that's just what happened when a dream turned out to be real.

"Be careful," the boy said. "Here, let me help you."

He pulled her to her feet, while she drank in each feature of his undeniably handsome face. He looked exactly as she remembered, right down to the cleft in his chin. His skin was warm and smooth and not at all freckled like hers was after a month of Minnehaha sun. His face was wide and friendly, and his nose was perfectly straight, except for a tiny bend at the tip, which was really only noticeable when he turned to the left. Perfect, rich brown bangs brushed across his eyebrows. And beneath them, blue eyes, so pale they were almost silver, shone on Sam—and only on Sam it seemed, nothing else.

Instantly all the fear Sam felt a few moments before was replaced by sheer joy. She burst into a wide, toothy smile, and the boy's smile grew brighter in return. Sam felt her tingles turn up from medium to high.

"You came!" he said. He seemed just as excited as she was, maybe even more. "Hi!" he went on. "I'm Dennis. Dennis Shaw."

"Uh . . ." Sam swallowed once, then twice, until she finally found her voice. "Hi. I'm so sorry. I was scared. I thought . . . Oh, never mind." She shook her head. "Hi," she repeated. "I'm Samantha." She breathed. "But everyone calls me Sam."

"Sam." He nodded, still grinning. "I like it. That's a really nice name." Then he paused as if he weren't quite sure what to say next. "You seem really nice too, Sam. I'm *so* glad you found my special place." He held out his arms wide. "What do you think? Isn't it great?"

Sam looked behind her at the treacherous pit and made a doubtful, *if you say so* face.

"Oh well." He shrugged apologetically. "I guess you're right," he said. He peered down into the hole. "How'd that get there, do you think?" Then he chuckled and reached a hand out to stroke the back of Sam's head. "Here. Let me help you get some of these leaves out of your hair."

She stood there, still, and let him. "Better?" she asked. She could feel his eyes studying her, then at last they met her own.

"Perfect." He grinned and nodded.

Sam caught her breath and tried to look down. She was blushing, she knew. And her insides felt all fizzy—like a soda that someone had shaken up. But her eyes stayed locked on his. She couldn't look away. Self-consciously she stood there, not sure what to do or what to say. Part of her wished that he'd stop staring, but part of her thought that it was great.

She waited for him to say something else, but all he did was smile.

Eager to break the tension, Sam pointed to the boy's red sweatshirt with the bold white letters across the front. "I see you're from Camp Hiawatha. I'm from Minnehaha," she proudly said.

"I know," he nodded, still smiling.

"You do?" she asked, surprised. She looked down at her own chest. There wasn't any writing on her T-shirt. *Hmm? How did he know that?*

"Well, yeah," he went on quickly. "I mean, there's not much else around here. Where else would you be from?"

"Oh, right." She giggled, feeling silly. *Relax, don't spoil it,* she told herself. *You don't get a second chance to make a first impression. Isn't that what her mom told her and Ali all the time?*

"So, is this your first summer at camp too?" she asked.

"Well, yes and no."

She felt a little silly, but she had to ask, "What does that mean?"

He smiled away the question. "So how do you like camp?"

"Oh, I *love* it!" she instantly gushed. "These four weeks went by so fast. I don't want to go home."

The boy's eyes grew a little wider. "Really?" He took her hand again. His grip was light and cool, but startlingly firm. "Hey, who knows?" he said somewhat breathlessly. "Maybe you won't!"

"Yeah, right." She felt her cheeks flush even redder. Every time he touched her, she felt a new shock. One thing was for certain, she knew: He wasn't like any boy she'd ever met.

"Come." He pulled her toward him.

"Huh?"

"Let me show you around."

"Okay." Sam nodded, still grinning.

She let him lead her across the grass to the little log cabin that, just like Dennis, was even cuter than in her dream. It was smaller than the bunks at camp—about half the size, in fact. And instead of thin flat boards, it was built entirely out of logs. Through the nearest window she could see two chairs and a table, also made of sturdy logs, and on the floor a sweet old-fashioned braided rug.

"So is this part of Camp Hiawatha?" she asked Dennis. *How cool for them,* she thought.

"Oh no." He shook his head. "It's kind of a secret. Most people don't even know it exists."

"Really?" She was surprised. "And they let you come here?" she asked.

"Uh . . ." He bit his lip. "No, not exactly." He shrugged

and tilted his head to one side. "Did they let *you* come here?"

"Well . . . no, not *exactly*." She couldn't help but grin a little wider. At the same time, though, she shivered as a chill ran up her spine. She rubbed her arms. They were covered with goose bumps. She guessed the sun was starting to go down. Then she realized with a panic that it *was*—and no, she *wasn't* supposed to be there at all. She didn't have time to stand there flirting. She really should be getting back!

"Oh, wow," she said. "You know, it's late. I really have to go."

"No, wait!" The smile drained instantly from Dennis's face. "Here! If you're cold, take this!" he said, and before she knew it he had his sweatshirt off and was holding it out. "Here! Hurry! Put it on!"

"Thank you." Surprised but grateful, Sam slipped her arms through the sleeves, then she zipped it up.

His smile was back, bright and eager. "Now you can stay here with me forever, if you want," he said.

The sweatshirt had instantly warmed her. She felt cozy and content. *I could stay here forever,* she thought. It would be just like in her dream, except she wouldn't have to wake up.

She could feel herself starting to nod.

But wait. No. She suddenly stopped.

What was she thinking? She shook the thought away. She couldn't *stay*. She had to go!

"I'm sorry, but I'll be in huge trouble if I don't get back soon. And hey, what about you?" she asked him. "Won't they be looking for you, too? I mean, you weren't planning to stay here all night by yourself, were you?"

He opened his mouth to reply, but then instead he took her hands. This time she actually jumped. The shock was double, at least, than the last time.

"Wow!" she said. "Sorry. I guess there's a lot of static electricity in the air."

"Oh, I wish you wouldn't go, Sam," he said solemnly.

She smiled as she disengaged her hands and begin to back away from the clearing. "I do too. But hey! There's a dance tonight, remember? I'll see you there in a few hours!"

CHAPTER 6

Letting go of Dennis Shaw's hands had been one of the hardest things she'd ever done, but as Sam made her return trip down the trail, she knew that she was right to head back to camp when she did and not stay a minute longer. In fact she probably should have gone back sooner, she realized, before the forest started getting so dark. The sun was still out, but now that it was setting in the late-August sky, the dapples of bright sunlight that had helped guide her before had all but disappeared. The woods were full of shadows now, and the path was harder to make out. She should have left a trail of crumbs like Hansel and Gretel, or she could have used friendship bracelet string. She had a whole trunkful, practically, back at camp.

This time through the woods, unfortunately, there was definitely no invisible force to help lead her along. Twice she was sure that she'd lost her way and would never get back. But then both times she stopped and took a deep breath and carefully retraced a few steps. And both times she looked down, relieved, to discover the ragged ribbon of path again.

At least she didn't feel cold, thanks to the thick red sweatshirt she'd forgotten to give back to Dennis. She'd been in such a hurry to go. She hoped *he* wasn't freezing, as she pulled the hood around her head. As soon as she did, its scent enveloped her and she had to close her eyes. It wasn't a strong smell exactly—just incredibly sharp and clear. There was the sweet perfume of the wildflowers and the tang of the cabin's pine walls. *There is even,* Sam thought with a shudder, *the dank, earthy odor of that dark hole.* And there was something else, something beneath all the other more familiar notes. She sniffed again, trying to place it. Was it Dennis himself? She wasn't sure. And that's when it suddenly hit her that she couldn't remember how he smelled. While all her other senses had been overloaded in his presence, that one alone had somehow been missed.

Well, I'll fix that problem tonight! Sam thought as she sighed dreamily and walked on.

At last she elbowed her way through a spindly thicket and found herself back on the Old Stump Trail. She broke into a trot and was back at camp, thankfully, just seconds before Kay rang the dinner bell.

Perfect, thought Sam. *I didn't miss anything!*

Her worries disappeared and were quickly replaced by happy relief. She still had ten whole minutes to get to the mess hall—just enough time, if she hurried, to get herself cleaned up and changed. The knees on her jeans were caked with dirt, and she had a feeling her face was too. She could feel where her needless tears had left stiff streaks along her cheeks. *I must look like such a mess,* she thought. Then she thought of Dennis—again—and smiled. She remembered how he'd said that she looked "perfect" when it couldn't have been further from the truth.

Well, if he didn't mind how I look now, she thought, *just wait till he sees me dressed up tonight!*

She couldn't think about Dennis without sighing and replaying every second with him in her head.

Sam. I like it. That's a really nice name . . .

You seem really nice too . . .

You can stay here with me forever . . .

Oh, I wish you wouldn't go . . .

She grinned, looking down at her hands and remembering how Dennis's had felt. She'd held a few boys' hands before, but they had never felt like his. *Did our hands really make sparks,* she wondered, *or did I just imagine it?* She rubbed them together and thought of how nice it would be to hold his hands again—and how she would in just a few hours. She could hardly wait to see him again—and introduce him to her friends! *Can I call him my boyfriend?* she wondered. She bit her lip and told herself yes.

Yes!

She couldn't believe it. A boyfriend. At last. It was something she'd always wanted—and one of the few things she hadn't yet had.

Oh, sure, lots of boys had liked her. That wasn't the problem at all. The problem was always that as soon as they liked her, she felt like moving on. But Dennis was different, that was obvious. It was just too bad that they'd met the last weekend of camp instead of the first. Then he could have been her boyfriend for the whole four weeks.

She walked on dreamily, holding his sweatshirt up to her nose.

"Sam!"

She stopped at the sound of her name and guiltily spun around.

"Oh, Gwen." She spotted her counselor. "Uh, hi. What's up?"

Gwen was seventeen and, as far as Sam was concerned, the best counselor in the world. From her cool beaded jewelry to her pretty, yet practical, French braids, she was just the kind of teenager that Sam hoped to be one day. Gwen wasn't smiling at her though. Beneath her khaki cap, she had a stern look on her face.

The counselor eyed Sam up and down. "I think what's up with *you* is the question," she replied. "Where have you been all afternoon? And what were you doing? You're a mess."

"Me? Um . . ." Sam wanted to look for somewhere small and dark to hide. "Well, I had arts and crafts and then swimming . . ." she started.

Gwen's eyebrows fell in together. "I'm talking about *after* that," she said. "Where exactly have you been for the past two *hours? Hmm?* Did you go off by yourself into the woods? And how'd you get so dirty? What'd you do? Fall in a trap?"

Sam wasn't sure if she turned red at that moment or as white as a ghost. What she did know was that she was sweating underneath the thick sweatshirt.

She took a deep breath. "Yes," she said, struggling to squeeze the meek sound out of her throat.

Gwen, meanwhile, shook her head, half in disappointment and half in dismay. "I can't believe it, Sam. What were you thinking? What if you'd gotten lost? Or hurt? Here I've been thinking you were counselor-in-training material, and you go and break a major Minnehaha rule."

Sam winced. Gwen's words hurt a lot—mostly because they were so true. She wanted to explain why it had been so worth it, but then she thought again. *I just had to meet this boy that I had a dream about.* She could imagine Gwen's reaction to that. Sam figured that the *whole* truth was probably best kept to herself.

The only thing Sam could do right now was beg for mercy. "I'm *so* sorry, Gwen. I am, *really*! Believe me, I can still be a good CIT." It was something she'd been thinking about since the first day of camp. Only a few girls got picked, and Sam was determined to be one. She thought about it every day.

The counselor sighed and looked down at her wrist full of colorful bracelets, at least half of which Sam had made. She straightened the knots on a few. "Well, I hope so," she said. "But I still have to punish you."

Sam closed her eyes and nodded. "I completely understand."

Gwen took a deep breath and crossed her arms. "I'm tempted to say no dance tonight, Sam," she declared.

What? No!

"I'm serious." Gwen nodded.

Sam's mouth fell wide open.

No! Anything but that!

"Oh, please, Gwen. *Please.* Can't it be something else? I'll clean the whole cabin. The latrine. Every bunk's latrine! Anything! Anything at all, if you'll only let me go."

"I don't know." Gwen pursed her lips and gave her chin a wary rub.

"Oh, please, Gwen," said Sam. "I'm so sorry. I really, really am."

"Sorry doesn't change the fact that you broke a rule,"

Gwen replied. But then her face softened slightly. "Oh, Sam, don't look at me like that."

Sam held her breath and hoped. Maybe, just maybe, Gwen would change her mind.

"Oh, okay. Maybe I'm being too harsh. You have been the perfect camper till now. And you did admit the truth when I asked you," Gwen went on.

Sam nodded and smiled weakly as her heart sputtered back to life.

"Plus I kind of like that latrine idea," Gwen said. "You know, someone let the toilet paper unravel all over the wet floor." She paused. "Okay, Sam, go clean it up, and I guess that's punishment enough. *This* time. Don't let there be a next time."

"Oh, Gwen! You're the best!" Sam reached out and hugged Gwen so hard that it knocked her hat onto the ground.

"Yeah, I know." Gwen grinned as Sam dove to retrieve the hat and returned it to her head.

"Thanks." Gwen reached up to straighten it, then her eyes grew serious again. "The thing is, Sam, this rule is no joke. It's *dangerous* to be out in the woods all by yourself. I mean, we try not to talk about it, but things have happened in the past." She eyed Sam's stained face and knees. "You didn't hurt yourself, did you?" she asked.

Sam wagged her head back and forth quickly. "No, no. Not at all. I'm fine."

"Hey." Gwen seemed to suddenly notice Sam's sweatshirt. "I didn't know you had one of those old Hiawatha sweatshirts. I haven't seen one of them in a while."

"Old?" Sam looked down self-consciously, but hopelessly happy, as well.

"You know, I don't know why they changed them and added a pine tree," Gwen went on. "I think the plain letters looked perfectly fine."

"When did they change them?" Sam asked. "Last year?"

Gwen shook her head. "Oh no. Gosh." She thought for a second. "It was before I even started coming here, so I'd say at least ten years ago. This one still looks pretty new, though." She gently brushed Sam's shoulder. "Except, of course, for all that dirt."

Sam shrugged, half smiling and wholly hoping that Gwen didn't ask her where the sweatshirt was from. At the same time, Sam had the very same question. She'd assumed it was Dennis's camp sweatshirt from this year.

But now it sounded like it couldn't be. She wondered where he'd gotten it. Just another question to ask him that night at the dance, it seemed.

The dance!

"What time is it?" Sam suddenly asked Gwen.

Gwen checked her watch. "Six o'clock."

Sam nodded toward the latrine. "Well, then I'd better get to work!"

Moments later another red-haired girl stepped out from behind the arts-and-crafts hut where she'd been hiding ever since Sam walked up. At first she'd been smiling. But not anymore. It was Ali, and from the moment Sam set off on her hike, she had been looking forward to seeing her sister squirm. It was because of Ali, in fact, that Gwen knew that Sam was gone. Gwen hadn't even asked. Ali just found her in the cabin and happily let the cat out of the bag. She couldn't remember the last time her sister had gotten in trouble, and it gave Ali goose bumps to watch Gwen chew her out. And then when she heard the counselor say "No dance," she was so thrilled she thought she'd burst!

But then, just like always, lucky-duck Sam came out

just fine. Ali was glad, at least, that she had walked away from that mess in the bathroom and left it for Sam to clean up—although Ali knew she could have made it much messier.

Ali knew that if *she'd* been caught doing what Sam did, she would have missed the dance for sure. She slept through one breakfast the first week of camp, and Gwen gave her a broom and made her sweep out the whole bunk.

How did Sam do it? That was all Ali wanted to know.

And why couldn't *she* lead Sam's charmed life, just for once.

CHAPTER 7

"Are you ready yet?" Ali asked, tapping her foot against the pale linoleum floor. "Everyone else is on the bus. If we don't go right now, they'll leave without us."

Sam spun around from the latrine mirror with an eager smile across her face. "Okay, I think I'm ready," she told her sister. "But first, be honest. How do I look?"

Ali shrugged. Sam looked amazing in her favorite green T-shirt, her cutest jeans, and the bead choker she'd made in arts and crafts that week. Her hair was held back with a thin glittery headband and hung past her shoulders in soft coppery waves. Ali had the instant urge to rip out her sparkly barrettes and do her hair the same way. But no, she could never give her sister that satisfaction. She left both barrettes in place, despising them with all her heart.

"You look fine," she told Sam dryly. "Anyway, it's too late to change."

"Okay." Sam sighed and grabbed a backpack off a nearby hook. "You're right. Let's go."

Ali eyed the bag. "What's in there?" she asked.

Sam hugged the backpack close and grinned. "Dennis's sweatshirt. I'm going to return it. Oh, and a brush. If you need it, just let me know."

Sam had told her sister *all* about Dennis, of course. But she'd decided to wait to tell the other girls in Bunk 9. She wanted to tell them—so badly!—but she was still self-conscious and even felt a little guilty about breaking the rules that afternoon. Plus she had had a whole latrine to clean while everyone else hung out talking and getting ready for the dance. She was actually glad that she didn't have time to answer any questions about where she'd been and what she'd done. And besides her friends would find out about her dreamy, amazing new *boyfriend*, Dennis Shaw, soon enough. (Surprising them at the dance was going to be so much fun!)

She wished that Ali seemed more excited for her, but at the same time, she wasn't surprised. She didn't know why awesome things that made her so happy always put Ali in such a bad mood.

What Ali *did* seem was curious. She kept asking question after question, like, "So what did he look like again?" and "What color were his eyes?" and "He wasn't at all creepy?" That one, in particular, she must have asked three times.

"No, he was nice!" Sam told her. "He was really sweet and cute!"

But instead of seeming satisfied, Ali frowned and looked confused.

The dance was in the boys' camp mess hall, which wasn't so different from the girls'. The floor, the walls, and the ceiling were all dark, well-worn wood, with thick timber columns running down the middle in two sturdy, spread-out rows. It had basically been transformed, though, by a big disco ball. The mirrored globe hung from a beam in the very middle of the room. A single spotlight was pointed at it. The hall was dark otherwise.

All the tables and benches had been pushed back to leave a wide-open space to dance, but it was still empty when the girls walked in and looked around. The boys hung back in the shadows by the benches, nodding and tapping their toes. The tiny lights cast by the disco ball were the only dancers so far. They swirled around the floor like tiny, cheerful ghosts.

"Well? Where is he?" Ali asked Sam, gazing around the hall.

Sam studied the scattered clusters of boys, in all their varying sizes and shapes. "I don't know. I don't see him yet," she whispered back. Her shoulders slumped in disappointment. "He'll get here later, I guess."

But how much later? Sam started to wonder as five, then ten, then fifteen minutes passed. It was dark, though. Could he be there and she didn't even know? Could she actually be missing that hair? And those eyes? She began to scour the room for a second, and soon a third, time.

By then a run of really good songs had gotten a few groups out onto the floor.

"Come on!" Jennifer said, running up to Sam and Ali. "Let's all go out and dance."

Ali sneered. "No thanks. I don't dance in groups."

Jennifer rolled her eyes. "Suit yourself," she told her. "How about you, Sam? Come on!"

"I will," Sam promised. "But not right now. You all go, and I'll meet you out there in a little while."

She watched her friends skip off together and let out a sigh. "Where *is* he?" she groaned to herself, looking all around.

But then, just at that very moment, Sam saw Ali's eyes grow wide. She was staring at something over Sam's shoulder. Sam instantly felt a flutter in her stomach as if she'd swallowed a little bird.

"Don't tell me this is *him*," Ali muttered, smirking.

Instantly Sam spun around. But where she first looked, there was nothing. Slowly her eyes drifted down. They landed eventually on a boy, but it wasn't Dennis. No. Definitely not.

This boy had short, bristly hair and a thick layer of freckles, and enormous, bright red ears.

"Hi. Want to dance?" he asked quickly, as if he were afraid he might forget.

Sam smiled down at him sweetly. "Me? Oh thanks! I would, but I'm actually waiting for someone right now. Hey, his name is Dennis. Do you know him?" she eagerly asked.

The boy nodded. "Yeah, sure. He's dancing with his girlfriend. Over there."

What?

Sam choked then coughed. It felt like a hammer had slammed her throat.

She followed his eyes across the dance floor as her whole body grew numb.

Beside her, Ali started laughing. *"Aww, poor Sam,"* she began to say.

Sam just kept peering. "Where is he?" she asked the boy.

"Right there," he said, pointing. "That's Dennis, there, with the blond hair."

"Oh!" Sam smiled and automatically began to breathe again. "Wrong Dennis!" She turned to Ali to share the happy news. Then she turned back to the boy and explained, "I meant Dennis *Shaw*."

"Oh, Shaw." The boy nodded.

"Yeah. Do you know him?" Sam asked.

The boy shook his head. "Nope. Sorry, I don't. I mean . . ." He paused to think, and Sam leaned toward him, waiting to hear what would come next.

"Yes?"

"I was just going to say the name does sound familiar. Shaw, I mean. I think some guys in my cabin had a counselor one year with that name. Hey, what cabin is your friend in?" he asked her.

"I don't know." Sam sucked her cheeks. She wished she'd thought to ask him that—along with so many other things. "But, I do know he's a camper here." She patted her backpack. "I have proof—a special sweatshirt that I have to return."

The boy, in the meantime, seemed to have only just noticed that Ali was standing there too. "Hey, are you guys twins?" he asked, cocking his head.

Ali rolled her eyes. "*No,*" she said, pulling her hair across her chin.

"Oh, Ali!" Sam laughed off her sister's sarcasm. Then she winked at her. "Hey, why don't *you* two dance? I'm going to keep looking for Dennis. You guys go out and have fun."

Ali glared at her smiling sister, but before she could say anything, they boy was dragging her away. He led her to the dance floor, where he immediately began to bob and sway. Ali cringed and closed her eyes so she didn't have to look at him. He reminded her of a sad, short-circuiting robot—with ridiculous satellite-dish ears.

Why didn't I dance with Jennifer and the other girls? she lamented to herself.

Meanwhile Sam's eyes were off again in search of Dennis, still with no success. There was a refreshment table, she could see, near the kitchen. Maybe Dennis was over there.

There was food laid out: some chips, and some cookies and brownies, which looked freshly made. Sam picked up one—a blondie, her favorite usually—and took a half-hearted bite. It tasted fine, but it didn't matter much since she had no appetite. All she could think about was Dennis Shaw. She wanted *him*, not something to eat.

You have to be patient, she tried to tell herself. *Maybe he stayed a lot longer in the clearing. And maybe he's still getting ready.* He might have wanted to take a shower. And hey, who knew? He might have run into his counselor and had some latrine cleaning to do too.

Sam took another brooding bite of the blondie. Then she noticed the wall behind the table. It was covered with old camp photographs. She walked around to look at them more closely. *It's better than just standing here looking stupid*, Sam told herself.

The photos, she saw, were of Hiawatha campers going all the way back to 1951. *Wow*, Sam thought. It was pretty amazing how alike the groups all looked. The only thing that really seemed to change was the haircuts—and color pictures, starting in 1974. Oh, and the sweatshirts, too, she realized. They had changed, just like Gwen said. The newer ones had a big pine tree encircled by the camp name on the front instead of a simple white CAMP HIAWATHA. The last year to have those, it looked like, was ten years ago. Sam's eyes wandered across the faces of that year . . . then suddenly stopped.

That face. That smile. Those eyes. They were so *familiar.* The sweatshirt, too. And instantly Sam knew why.

They all belonged to Dennis Shaw!

But, no. Of course it *couldn't* be. The picture was ten years old. There was no possible way that Dennis could be in it. *That would make him an adult by now!* Sam thought.

Still, the resemblance between them was unbelievable, and it sent a chill zipping straight up her spine. She wished she could turn on the lights in the mess hall and get a better, clearer look. If only there were names on that year, as there were on a few other ones.

Names!

Of course! Why hadn't she looked at those before?

There was no picture for this year's group yet, but

there was for the year before. And yes, there were names for that year. She scanned them.

And yes, there was a Shaw!

Sam sighed, though. It wasn't Dennis. This boy's name was Ben. And he looked older, like a counselor, though his eyes were the same silvery blue like Dennis's. She traveled back to the year before that one and found a slightly younger Ben again. And this time he wasn't the only Shaw. There was *another* one named Nick. In fact, of all the pictures with names, she quickly realized, at least half had one Shaw or more—and the resemblance between all of them was amazingly strong.

Ah, that's it! Sam thought. That picture from ten years ago wasn't of Dennis. It was of his brother, or some young uncle, or cousin. Whatever. That wasn't the point. The point was, this camp was full of Shaws, or at least had been in the past. And *that* explained everything, as far as Sam was concerned: the picture, the old sweatshirt, and how Dennis knew about that secret cabin hidden away deep in the woods. It even explained why he answered both yes and no when she asked him if it was his first summer at camp. *His family has been coming here forever—he must feel like he's a part of this place and this place is a part of him.*

It all made perfect sense now, and Sam couldn't help but smile.

I'd make a pretty good detective, Sam thought, *if I do say so myself.*

If only she could solve the mystery of where Dennis was *now*, and why he was keeping her waiting, she'd feel 100 percent better.

She hoped his feelings hadn't changed since she'd left him in the woods.

The sudden thought drained her smile.

What if he had changed his mind and didn't really like her that much after all?

She stuffed the rest of her blondie in her mouth, then anxiously wiped her hands. That's when the feel of a hand on her back made her instantly spin around.

"Dennis!" she cried—and a mouthful of blondie spewed out into space.

CHAPTER 8

Jennifer laughed. "Oh, Sam! I'm so sorry! I didn't mean to startle you!" She brushed the pale, sticky crumbs off the front of her shirt. Her face was already flushed from dancing, and her dirty blond hair was damp. Strands clung to her neck in soggy ropes, and a few crossed her cheeks like shiny scars. She pried them off with her fingers, then crossed her arms and scratched at two angry bugbites on her elbow.

"So, who's *Dennis*?" she asked, raising her eyebrows. "Is *he* why you haven't been dancing? What's up?"

Sam bit her lip. *Do I tell her?* she wondered. Suddenly, she wasn't sure. The part of her that was still excited about having a *boyfriend* wanted to tell her friend everything. But the part that was starting to lose hope in his coming wanted to tell her to forget it.

But before Sam could say anything, her sister came skulking up.

"So how was your dance?" Sam asked Ali. "That guy seemed really nice."

Ali rolled her eyes. "Oh, just dreamy," she grumbled, then she faked a squinty smile.

"Well, here, have a cookie." Sam held out a plate. "They have your favorite. Chocolate chip."

Ali took one, then she grabbed one more as Sam put back the plate. "Thanks, Sam. You're so very kind to offer me the ones you don't want . . . just like boys," she said between sour bites.

"Huh?" Sam stared at her sister, bewildered. She knew her sister was shy about asking boys to dance, and how bored she always got at their dances at school—so why was Ali so upset now, Sam wondered, when all she had done was try to help her have a little fun?

Jennifer, meanwhile, ignored Ali and focused her attention instead on Sam. "I still want to know why you're hanging out all by yourself, Sam, and who this Dennis guy is!" She peered over Sam's shoulder at the wall of photos. "Is he in one of these pictures?" she asked.

"Hey, guys! Jennifer! You left us!" squealed Megan, running up just then to join them. Stefi and Georgia were close behind. They were all glowing with excitement and giddy from almost an hour of jumping around nonstop.

"Mmm! Snacks!" said Stefi, grabbing a brownie.

Georgia eyed the bowl of chips and took a handful. "Just what I needed!" She grinned. "Then I'm going to ask that guy to dance!" She pointed a chip at a tall boy by the door to the kitchen. "I think he's been checking me out since we got here."

The girls followed her gaze.

"Who?" Ali said. "That guy with the blond hair?"

"Mmn-hmn!" Georgia chewed noisily and grinned.

Ali snorted. "Ah, yeah. Good luck with that."

Georgia's eyebrows slid bitterly together. "Oh, who asked you, Ali?" she said.

"Whatever," said Ali. "But he has a girlfriend, just so you know."

Georgia turned to Sam, who shrugged and nodded.

"She's right," Sam said.

"Aw. No fair!" Georgia whined. Then she looked around quickly, waving a half-eaten chip. "Okay. So I guess I'll just find someone else."

Just then a group of boys burst through the mess hall doors, and Sam stood up on her tippy-toes to try to check them out.

Was Dennis with them? No. They were too young. Probably fifth graders. *Too bad . . .*

Ali followed Sam's eyes. "Don't even *think* about setting me up with one of those little twerps," she snapped.

Georgia whipped her head around to see. "Well, you know, you can't be too picky, Ali, when you refuse to dance in a big group with us."

Ali crossed her arms. "I just don't get the point."

"Duh!" Megan frowned at her. "The point is to have fun."

"Right." Jennifer nodded. "But remember who you're talking to," she said.

Ali cut her eyes to Jennifer. "What does that mean?" she asked.

"Nothing." Jennifer shrugged. "It just means that you don't seem that interested, most of the time at least, in having fun."

"Oh, Ali has fun sometimes," said Sam.

Jennifer turned to her. "She does? Really? How?"

"Well . . ." Sam tried to think, then she turned to her sister, at last. "What *do* you like, Ali?" she asked.

Ali huffed. "You know what I like?" She shot a look at each of the girls from Bunk 9. "I like people to leave me alone. You guys don't know the first thing about me. Not even you, Sam," she said.

Sam stared back at her, stunned, and Ali thought about saying even more. Things like: *Think about it, Sam. You don't know what I like to do or what I'm interested in. And you never ask because you don't care. You go around acting like the whole world revolves around you, and you have since we were little. Maybe just once in your life you could think about someone besides yourself.* But instead she bit her lip so hard she could taste the tang of her blood.

"Well, why don't we leave her alone," said Georgia, wiping her hands on the legs of her jeans.

"Yeah, I love this song," said Megan. "If you don't want to dance, that's your problem, Ali."

"Come on!" Jennifer tugged on Sam's elbow. "The dance'll be over soon."

Sam sighed. "Oh, I don't know."

"What is *wrong* with you?" Stefi asked.

Ali rolled her eyes impatiently. "Oh, why don't you

just tell them? Enough drama already, Sam."

"Tell us what?" The other girls crowded around Sam even closer.

"Well—" Sam began.

"That she was hoping to meet some guy here at the dance," said Ali, "but he hasn't shown up yet."

"Really?" Megan made a sad face. "Aw, bummer!" She laid her arm across Sam's shoulders and gave her a sympathetic squeeze.

"Hey, he could still come," Stefi said. "Right? I mean, the dance isn't over *yet*."

"Oh, face it," said Ali. "He's not coming." She looked Sam squarely in the eye. "You got stood up," she said. The words felt so good as they came out. "I guess he didn't like you as much as you thought."

"Oh!" Now it was Jennifer's turn to glare at Ali. "What a terrible thing to say!"

"Yeah," said Georgia. "Even if it's true, you don't have to be so harsh, Ali."

"I'm sure it's *not* true," said Stefi.

"Totally not," Megan agreed. "But still. That doesn't mean we have to just stand around here. Come on." She grabbed one of Sam's hands and nodded to Jennifer, who took the other one. "This is the best song, and we sure don't need boys to dance to it. Whenever Dennis gets here, Sam, he'll find you, don't worry—and when he does, he should see you having fun!"

And with that, the girls herded Sam out onto the dance floor, leaving Ali all alone. She watched the disco lights swirl over the girls as if to sweep them up. Soon a group of boys joined them, along with the girls from Bunk 10. Ali could see Sam's smile grow brighter, and her own hands clenched in fists. First Sam broke the rules and still got to come. Then the boy from her dream—who was *real*—stands her up, and she still has fun. Ali, meanwhile, said one little thing—that was totally true—and the girls turned their backs on her. *Well, I never liked them anyway,* she told herself, *so why should I care?* There was only one thing that really mattered to her for the rest of the night: Whoever this guy Dennis was, he'd better not show up.

CHAPTER 9

The next morning, a sunny Saturday, there were mixed emotions in Bunk 9. Jennifer, Georgia, Megan, and Stefi were all still giddy from the dance the night before. Ali, on the other hand, was still bitter because the only people—other than the girls from her bunk—who had talked to her all night were people who thought that she was Sam. (Then, of course, as soon as they realized who she really was, they all found some quick excuse to hurry off.) But Ali was also satisfied to know that Sam's luck had finally run out. Dennis, the boy Sam had waited for, never did appear, and Ali couldn't help but enjoy the sight of her sister sulking, for once in her charmed life on the verge of heartbroken tears.

"I can't believe today's our last full day," said

Jennifer. "What do you think we should do?"

They'd just come back from breakfast and were stretched out on their bunks. Gwen had suggested they start packing, but that was the last thing anyone wanted to do. There would be a big end-of-session camp color war beginning at one o'clock, but until then they were free to do whatever they wanted, just about.

None of them had been in a color war before, but Gwen had explained it to them earlier. Together with Bunks 1 and 5 they would be Team Red, and all afternoon they'd compete against other color teams in a dozen or so events. There'd be team sports, like volleyball and basketball, as well as some individual ones (which was great for Team Red since Sam was the best archer in all of Minnehaha). There'd also be a team cheer competition and a big relay race at the end, and some other surprise games that they didn't even know about yet. At the end the team with the most points would get special trophies, but that wasn't the best part. The winners would also get to have their trunks packed for them by their counselors.

"It's already hot," said Megan, fanning herself, as she lay back on her bunk. "I say we go to the pool."

"Hey, good idea!" Georgia sprang up and began to

look for her bathing suit. "I just *have* to do a back flip off that diving board before I go home."

"You haven't done one yet?" scoffed Ali.

Georgia took a deep breath and shook her head. "No."

"And have *you*, Ali?" said Jennifer. "I sure haven't seen you, if you have."

Ali turned away. "Oh really? That's too bad for you, I guess."

"Well, let's all go and you can show us, Ali!" said Stefi. She kissed Bingo and propped him up just so. Then she jumped down off her bunk. "Come on." She looked up at Sam, who was still lying back, legs crossed. "What are you waiting for, Sam? Hey, you're not still thinking about that dumb guy from Camp Hiawatha, are you?"

"Yeah, forget about him," said Megan. "I mean, I'm sure he was sick, but still, he should have gotten a message to you."

"What? No." Sam shook her head quickly. "I'm over his spell! Just feeling lazy." She grinned and patted the paperback beside her. "You guys go ahead without me," she said. "I'm going to save my energy for the color war and just hang out and finish this book."

"Aw!" Stefi frowned, and so did the others. "Really?" she said.

"Yeah, *really?*" said Ali, leaning out from her bunk to try to see her sister's face. That had to be the first time ever that Sam felt "lazy." Or passed up swimming with her friends.

"Yeah, *really.*" Sam grinned. "Go ahead." And with that she opened her book. "Have fun, you guys. And good luck with that flip, Georgia. I know you can do it."

As soon as they'd all changed and had left, Sam started reading, but she didn't read for very long. She waited till Ali had gone too—not to the pool, but to the latrine. By then she was sure the other girls had reached the pool and weren't coming back for a forgotten towel or sunscreen. Then she hopped down out of her bunk and grabbed her backpack off her hook. She opened the cabin door, slipped out, and headed toward the woods.

She just had to do it. She knew she shouldn't, but she couldn't help herself. She had a good hour and a half, she figured, to hike to the clearing and back. It was more than enough time to leave the sweatshirt and return to camp before she was missed. And this time there'd be no worry that Gwen would ask anyone where she was. All the counselors were way too busy getting ready for the color war later on. The only question in Sam's mind was, would Dennis be there again?

And maybe one more, she admitted: Did she want to see him if he was?

Of course she was dying to know why he hadn't been at his own camp's dance the night before. Especially when he knew that she'd be there—and when it had seemed that he liked her so much. Had she been totally wrong about that? (And had Ali been right?) Or was there a perfectly good explanation? If there was, she wanted to know. And if there wasn't, well then she kind of wanted to know that, too. And if Dennis Shaw *didn't* like her, then she definitely didn't want his dumb sweatshirt.

She made her way to the Old Stump Trail, happy at once for the shade. It wasn't as cool as a swim, but it was still a relief from the surprisingly early heat of the late August day. As she walked, she kept her eye out for the trail marker and the spot where the path to the clearing began. There, just ahead, she saw it and took it, weaving through the leafy tree limbs. She wasn't as worried this trip as the last one about getting lost or losing the trail. She remembered how it zigged and zagged in places and recognized a few trees here and there, and it was early and the sun was high and bright and clearly not going anywhere. Plus this time Sam had brought her compass with her and even her map. *Why waste four weeks of orienteering?* she'd thought when she tucked them in her bag. She didn't pull them out, though. She didn't have to. Once again the trail was surprisingly easy to follow, considering it was barely there. And the farther she went, the more strongly it pulled her, step by step by step. Her heart was beating fast and only got faster as she moved along.

At last, like a lighthouse, a ray of bright sun signaled that the clearing wasn't too far ahead. Sam reached it and pushed through the last prickly thicket, prepared to feel the sun again. But she didn't. To her surprise the clearing was every bit as cool and maybe even cooler than the trail. And the pleasant smell she remembered was replaced by a sweet, moldy smell, like a pile of leaves in the fall. The sweetness almost stung her nose. The grass was so dead it looked like hay. *Everything looked so much more alive yesterday,* she thought.

A shiver shot up her spine suddenly, and instinctively she rubbed her arms. Then she held them out and looked down. She could *see* the sun shining down on them, but they were covered with goose bumps. She thought of the sweatshirt in her backpack and considered putting it on. But no. It wasn't hers. She'd come to give it back.

So, is Dennis here? she wondered, scanning the clearing. It was so quiet and still. Even the butterflies seemed to be resting, barely moving their papery wings. Sam listened and realized her breathing was the loudest thing in the whole place. Or was it her heart steadily thumping away between short breaths? She was almost afraid to break the silence by calling out Dennis's name. She opened her mouth, then she closed it and decided to walk up to the cabin and peek inside instead.

If he was there, great. Then maybe he could explain. But if not, fine. She'd leave the sweatshirt there for him to find when—and if—he came back.

This time, Sam watched where she was going and was careful to stay clear of any holes. She stuck to the grass and made a wide circle around any suspicious patches of leaves. Now and then she looked over her shoulder, not exactly sure why. She hoped to see Dennis, but she didn't. Nor did she see anyone else. And yet, it sure felt as if eyes were on her, carefully watching her every step.

Snap!

The sudden sound of something breaking made Sam jump and spin around. Then she spotted the twig beneath her shoe. *Relax,* she told herself. *It was nothing, Sam, only you.*

At last she reached the cabin and stood outside the door. It looked more dilapidated than she remembered it being yesterday. Her crush on Dennis must have blinded her. She could knock, she guessed, but she was sure by then that no one was inside. If Dennis was there, he would have seen her—or heard her—by now and come out. A sinking, hollow feeling told her she'd come here for nothing. She had no boyfriend, after all. She took a deep breath, full of disappointment, and slowly let it out.

There was an old, weathered latch on the door, and she lifted it. She reached for the handle, about to pull. But it hurt—"Ow!" she cried, letting go.

The handle was so cold that it burned!

Stunned and stinging, Sam winced and stood there. Then suddenly her eyes grew wide.

The door before her was swinging open . . .

Cr-e-e-eaaak . . .

All by itself.

CHAPTER 10

Too stunned to scream, Sam fell back and landed on the grass. Still she kept her eyes on the doorway, sure that something awful was about to jump out. The door was open just a fraction, so she couldn't see inside. She could make out only shadows. Was that the chair? She couldn't tell. Not only was it dark in the cabin, it was murky, as well. It was as if the place were filled with smoke. Sam sniffed, ready to smell the acrid odor, but something quite different met her nose. She inhaled again. It was familiar. She knew she'd smelled it before, and she was just beginning to remember where, when suddenly she heard the groan of a loose floorboard.

She scrambled back, prepared to jump up and run, but her feet slid on the slick grass. She lay there, splayed out, as the floor groaned once again. Then it stopped, and there was a *cr-e-e-eaaak*. . . .

The door was opening all the way.

Out of the shadows, a figure appeared . . . and Sam felt dizzy with relief.

It was Dennis. He stepped out and stood above her, smiling, and offered her his hand. "I'm sorry. I didn't mean to scare you. Are you okay? Here."

Sam closed her eyes for moment and let her heart relax. Then finally she took his hand. A tingle stung her the instant that their fingertips met. "Ouch!" she gasped.

"Sorry," she mumbled as she let him gently help her to her feet. The sting had died away. Sam realized she wasn't so mad anymore; she was far more embarrassed. She'd only seen Dennis twice so far, and both times he'd found her on the verge of freaking out. She hated to imagine what a timid, nervous, scaredy-cat he thought she was.

She tried to laugh as she stood there brushing the back of her shorts. "You must think I'm such a spaz. I swear, I'm not usually this jumpy," she said. "Seriously. I *love* haunted houses!"

"You do?" He gazed at her and grinned.

"Oh yeah. The scarier the better. And scary movies,

too. My sister and I watch them all time—well, not at camp, of course. It might be the only thing we have in common." She thought of Ali and wrung her hands. "Anyway, I just want you to know, I usually have a *very* high tolerance for fear," she told Dennis. Then she looked around and humbly smiled. "I guess there's just something about feeling like you're all alone out here in the woods. Do you know what I mean?"

He slowly nodded in reply. The corners of his mouth were still turned up, but the smile had drained from his eyes. "I do," he said, very softly. "That's why it's so great that you came back."

"Yeah?" Sam could feel herself blushing. The words sounded so nice. But they also made her confused. "You know, I looked for you at the dance last night," she told him. "I waited and waited, thinking you'd come. I mean . . ." She looked down at her feet. "Yesterday it sounded like you liked me. Remember all those things you said? But then, well, when you weren't at the dance, all I could think was I had it all wrong."

"But I *do* like you!" he said quickly.

"Well, you have a funny way of showing it," she said.

"I'm really, *really* sorry. *Really* sorry," he replied.

Sam waited for more information. A good excuse would have been nice. But it didn't seem to be coming. "Well, where *were* you?" she finally asked.

His eyes left her for the first time to stare, slightly puzzled, into space. Then they returned, and he rubbed his middle. "Stomach," he explained. "It must have been the meatballs. I thought I was going to die," he joked.

"Really?"

He nodded.

"Meatballs?"

"Well I guess it could have been anything." He shrugged. "It wouldn't be the first time either, by the way," he went on. "You think being in the woods by yourself is scary, try eating the food at Hiawatha sometime."

"The blondies weren't bad," she told him.

"Well, then I'm sure they had those brought in. Believe me." He leaned in closer and took her hands in his. "If I *could* have been there, Sam, I would have. But there was just no way on earth."

A spark zipped through her once more, and she paused to let it settle down. Finally, she found her own smile. "Then I'm glad you're better now."

So he *hadn't* stood her up. Ali had been wrong. The thought warmed her from the inside. She wasn't half as chilly anymore.

"I'm really sorry, Sam," he told her. He lightly squeezed her hands. "I wanted to see you, and if I could have been there, I would have. I swear."

"I wish I'd known." Sam sighed. "You know, I asked about you. I thought I'd find someone who knew you. But it was weird. No one did."

He cocked his head. "Really? That *is* weird," he said. But his shrug seemed to say that he didn't really care. "They were probably just pranking you," he added.

"I did see your picture, though," said Sam.

"My picture?" His ardent smile disappeared.

She giggled. "It wasn't really your picture. But some relative who looks just like you, I guess."

"Oh." He nodded slowly, though he still looked unsure.

"I'm talking about the camp pictures, you know? In the mess hall? There was one guy who looked *exactly* like you from ten years ago. You must know who I'm talking about. Who was it?" she asked. "Your older brother? It looked like Hiawatha's had a *lot* of Shaws, hasn't it?"

"Yeah, you can say that again." Dennis's voice was

flat, his face without expression. "You can also say that when you're a Shaw, you don't have much choice about it. I tried to put off coming as long as I could, but my parents finally made me. So I guess I showed them." He was still holding Sam's hands, but he seemed to have forgotten she was there. Then he suddenly caught her staring. "Huh, sorry." He coughed and grinned. "Who cares about Shaws and all that stuff? Let's talk about *us*, Sam," he said.

Us. Sam couldn't help it. Her knees felt instantly weak. She'd never been part of an "us" talk before, and it sounded so sweet.

"You're very special, Sam," Dennis told her. His voice was cheerful once more, but intense. "I like you a lot. Tell me, can you see us being together forever? Because I can," he declared.

Sam was speechless. *Together. Forever.* The words were too much to take in. But Dennis didn't seem to need an answer.

"I know! Let me make the dance up to you tonight," he said.

"Tonight?"

"Yes. It'll be perfect. Tonight's the full moon. We can

have our *own* dance. Just you and me, Sam. It'll be so much fun!"

"Yes!" came out of her mouth before she could think of the reasons for "no." But as soon as it did, she bit her lip. Sneak out tonight for a dance in the middle of the woods? It was absolutely, positively, completely ludicrous.

"What's wrong?" Dennis asked.

"Oh, well, you know." She smiled weakly. "It's just *soooo* against the rules."

"So?"

Sam gazed up, not sure if his voice had asked the question or if it had only been his eyes.

So, she thought, *if Gwen or anyone finds out, I will be in the biggest trouble of my life.*

She wouldn't be sent home, of course, since her parents were coming the very next day. But what would they say when they found out? Sam would surely be grounded for what was left of the summer and probably for the rest of her life! And what would the camp do? She wouldn't get to be a CIT, that was for sure. She might not even get to come back next summer. The risks were obviously huge. But then, as Dennis gazed at her with his mesmerizing eyes, another thought pushed that one aside. Sam had spent her whole life obeying rules and doing "the right thing." Maybe now it was finally time to start following her heart. The one and only rule she'd broken had led her to Dennis after all. And how often did you meet a sweet, gorgeous boy who could imagine being together *forever* with you? Not very often!

Of course, it was hard to imagine how that would work. Where did he live, anyway? Sam almost asked. But what did it matter? she decided. That was something they could talk about while they danced in the moonlight. All she had to do now was give him an answer.

"Okay," she said. "I'll do it." The tingling had spread through her whole body by now. "I'll come," she declared. "But it'll have to be late. Today we have a color war, then a campfire tonight, and a cookout and awards."

"The later the better," he assured her. "I'll be waiting. Just be sure to come."

She nodded slowly, knowing that time was passing quickly and she really should return to camp. She slipped her hands out of his reluctantly and took a half step back.

"Oh, I almost forgot," she said. "Your sweatshirt. Here." She pulled the bulky red bundle out of her backpack and offered it to him. "That's why I came, actually, to return it."

"Keep it," he said, smiling back. "In fact," he went on, "you can keep it forever, if you want."

"Are you sure?" asked Sam. "I know they don't make them like this anymore, and your brother might want it back."

"My brother? Oh right." He nodded, then pointed to the ground. "Hey, looks like you dropped something."

Sam followed his gaze and sure enough saw her compass lying in the grass.

"Oops! Thanks! It must have fallen out of my bag when I pulled out the sweatshirt." She scooped it up and glanced at the face. "Oh no," she groaned. The tiny metal needle was whirling like a top. She tapped it gently, but it just kept spinning. "Aw, it's broken. Look." She sighed and showed it to him. "I hope I don't need it to get back to camp," she joked.

He laughed a little and nodded. "Or to get back here tonight."

Then he bent down and picked a flower and gently tucked it behind her ear. "Until tonight," he said. "I'll be waiting for you, right here."

CHAPTER 11

Sam left the clearing—and Dennis—in what could only be called a daze. Her heart was jumping around inside her, while her mind was filled with a single, buzzing thought: the moonlit dance she'd soon share with dreamy Dennis Shaw! She reached up and slipped the flower he'd given her out from behind her ear. She held it to her nose and closed her eyes and breathed it in. She sighed. It was like being in the clearing with him all over again. She inhaled one more time, then carefully set it back in place.

Gradually it came to her that she needed to pay attention and make sure she didn't lose the trail. It was early and so sunny that she wasn't too worried—but still. Now that her compass was broken, she couldn't count on it for help. She looked around to get her bearings and assured herself that, yes, she was going the right way. Then her mind was free to go back to looking forward to that night.

What should she wear? she wondered. The same green shirt she wore last night? Yes, definitely. But maybe instead of wearing her hair down she would try to put it up. It would be hard of course to get ready after lights-out, when everyone else was in bed. She would just have to do her best, she guessed. Oh, and she'd have to remember to bring a pen and paper so she could write down his e-mail address. Then they could write each other and chat every day when they got home. She wondered where he lived and if it was close enough that they could see each other before next summer, when they got back to camp. Being *together forever* was going to be tricky, she realized, if he lived too far from where she did.

She drifted down the narrow trail breezily, knowing she could go faster and probably should. She shifted her backpack and looked up at the tiny skylight of sun peeking through the tall ceiling of trees. It was impossible to tell what time it was, but she was doing fine. She hoped she was at least.

And then, as if out of nowhere, a thick gray cloud rolled over the sun. The light that had highlighted the trail for her suddenly disappeared. It was replaced by murky shadows and an uneasy chill. Sam shivered and looked around at the now gloomy forest. It had been so pleasant just a split second before. But now it felt cold and dark and lonely—and even a little dangerous.

Sam realized she'd stopped breathing and took a nervous gulp of air. *Stay calm. Clouds come,* she told herself. *They pass. It's no big deal.*

She picked her way through the overgrowth a little farther, but the clouds didn't move on. In fact, they grew even thicker, and the dim light faded more. Slowly but surely the whole forest seemed to turn an uneasy shade of greenish gray. Her feet got caught again and again on thick roots that were impossible to spot. She wished she had a flashlight, but who in their right mind would have thought to bring one in the middle of the day?

Sam wasn't a nail biter; still she began to gnaw them just the same. Then she remembered Dennis's sweatshirt and pulled it out and slipped it on. There. That made her feel a little better. At least it reminded her of the happy clearing and helped to warm her up.

She forged on and tried to keep her mind on *that* instead of on how creepy and even scary the forest around her had become. After all, hadn't she just told Dennis how "brave" she really was? It was just the woods. And it was early. *What's there to be afraid of?* she thought. But as she anxiously looked around, she couldn't help but think, *A lot.*

There was no way to ignore the phantomlike trees or their spindly branches. They swiped at her like claws. And there was no way not to imagine a million . . . *somethings* . . . in the shadows watching her.

Sam could feel the downy hairs on her neck bristling, standing defensively on end. In her chest her heart was pounding so hard she was afraid it might bruise her ribs. At last, without even deciding to, she broke into a run. *You're being silly!* she told her legs. But they weren't listening to her.

She hurdled over ferns and bushes, weaving in and out of trees until—*"Agh!"*—her toe caught on something hard, and she tumbled to her knees. Immediately she jumped up and began to run again. *Where is that Old Stump Trail? Please let it be close!* she thought.

Wait! Was it there? Just ahead? Where the shadows

seemed to even out? She lunged for it, hoping with all her heart that she was right. But the next thing she knew, she tripped again. She had no idea on what. All she knew was it sent her stumbling off the path and into an enormous, thorny bush.

"*Ugh!*" Sam groaned as she struggled to free herself. With all her wriggling her compass slipped out of the sweatshirt's pocket. Sam contorted herself so that she could pick it up. Broken or not, looking at it filled her with memories.

"Got it!" Sam grunted triumphantly. She noticed that it was no longer spinning wildly, but she didn't have time to wonder what that meant.

"*Ouch!*" she cried. Her hair was stuck!

She reached back to try to free it from a knot of inch-long barbs. *That was stupid,* she thought. Almost instantly she pricked her finger on the longest, sharpest one. She was sure that she was bleeding. She could feel the pooling drops. Then she felt something else. It was dry, but sticky . . .

Ew!

And it was everywhere!

"*Aggghhh!!!!*"

Sam wasn't just caught in a bush. She was in an enormous spiderweb.

Her arms flailed and so did her legs, terrified that the huge eight-legged monster who'd woven the web was still in it with her. She scrambled to her feet and pawed at herself mercilessly, desperate to strip off each and every thread. She could hear herself screaming and kept going until her throat was raw. She finally stopped, but she was still shuddering. Exhausted, she staggered back toward the path. She saw the gap in the trees and felt a tidal wave of relief. Yes! The Old Stump Trail.

She sighed and let her head fall back. There in the sky was a small dot of blue. And then, almost as swiftly as they came, the clouds began to move away. The sun seemed just as relieved as Sam and happy to make up for lost time. Every leaf seemed to suddenly sparkle, and the trail was clear and bright. Sam hurried forward without looking back, eager to leave the last quarter mile of her life behind.

And that's when she felt the yank on her sweatshirt that stopped her dead in her tracks.

CHAPTER 12

"*Ali!* You scared me!" Sam shrieked.

"I did?" Ali stood there with her hand still gripped tightly around Sam's hood. "Oh sorry." She smiled and let go. "I didn't mean to," she said. "Sounded to me like you were pretty scared already. Was that you I heard screaming?"

Sam straightened her sweatshirt, smoothed her hair back, and tried to look as composed as she possibly could. "I just tripped and fell in a spiderweb, and I guess I got a little freaked out, that's all. Anyway, what are you doing here?" She gave Ali a suspicious frown.

Ali crossed her arms in front of her. "Isn't that what I should be asking *you?*" she replied. She eyed her sister warily. "I *knew* you didn't want to stay in the cabin this morning just so you could sit there and read. *Especially* on the last day. You're so into your friends and everything. And sure enough, when I came back to the cabin you were gone."

"How'd you know where I went?" Sam asked her.

"It wasn't hard. Where else would you go but off into the woods by yourself? I bet to try to see that boy." She clicked her tongue and shook her head. "You know"—she lowered her chin menacingly—"the 'model camper' part of me kind of thinks that I should really tell Gwen."

Instantly a whole new terror froze Sam's blood in her veins all over again. "Oh no! No, you can't, Ali! Please, don't!" she begged. "I'll do anything. Anything in the whole world! I swear."

Ali's mouth slid to the side. Thoughtfully she rubbed her chin. She hadn't even planned to blackmail her sister. She'd just meant to make her sweat. But it was certainly too good an opportunity to waste now, that was for sure.

She thought for a second. What did she want from Sam anyway? Nothing, really—except to feel just once that she was just as good as her.

"Well?"

"I'm *thinking*," said Ali. She squared her shoulders. "Okay. How about for the rest of the day you trade places with me?"

"What do you mean?" Sam asked.

"What do you mean, what do I mean? I mean you be me and I be you. It won't be hard. We *are* twins."

Sam tilted her head. "Uh . . . yeah . . . but . . ."

Ali nodded and forced a tight grin. Then she pointed to Sam's chin.

Sam touched it lightly. Her skin felt stiff, and a little sticky, too. *Ah,* she thought, looking down at her wounded finger. In her frenzy she must have smeared her chin— and who knew what else—with her own blood.

"Does it look like your birthmark?" she asked Ali.

Ali nodded. "Pretty much." But then she took hold of Sam's finger and gave the tip a tight squeeze. A bright crimson drop oozed out. Ali took it and rubbed it over Sam's chin just below where the dried blood stopped.

"There," she said with satisfaction. "That'll do, I think. I doubt anyone looks at me closely enough to care if it's perfect anyway." Then she stroked her own chin. "A little makeup and *voilà!* We'll be good to go."

"But *why?*" Sam asked. She'd been expecting Ali to

say, *Take me to the mall with your friends when we get home,* or ask for her birthday money at least. Trading places for a day seemed fun in a movie or TV show, but a little strange in real life.

"Does it matter?" said Ali. "Just tell me if we have a deal or not." She crossed her arms again.

Sam felt the stain on her chin again. The new blood was still sticky and damp. Well, what choice did she have, she realized. If she said no, Ali would tell Gwen. And not only would she risk leaving camp in disgrace, she'd miss seeing Dennis again.

Dennis . . .

Sam couldn't help but break into a smile as his handsome face filled her mind.

"What?" Ali frowned. "Do you think it's so funny?"

Sam shook her head. "No, it's not that. I'm sorry. I was just thinking about, well . . ." She sighed. "*Him.* He *was* there, Ali! Dennis! Oh, you have to meet him. He's *so* sweet and nice." She reached up to pat the flower he'd given her. But it had fallen out when she fell. She touched the empty spot anyway and dreamily closed her eyes. *That's okay,* she thought. *He'll give me another one tonight.*

She opened her eyes to find Ali scowling.

"Nice enough to stand you up?" said Ali.

"No, that's the thing," Sam explained. "He *didn't*. He was *sick*! I knew there was a good reason. He said he ate some bad meatballs. Poor guy. I felt so bad for him."

"Oh." was all Ali could say, her blood starting to boil.

"And that's not all," Sam went on, unable to keep it all in. "Guess what else he said?"

"What?" Ali asked, though she knew she didn't really want to hear.

"He said he wanted to make it up to me by having another dance!"

"Another dance?" Ali scowled. "What are you talking about?"

"Tonight! In his special place," gushed Sam. "Just the two of us under the full moon!"

"Really." Ali's arms pressed into her ribs, and she bit the soft inside of her cheeks hard.

"Yes! He told me to come back tonight, and he'd be there waiting for me because, get this: He wants to be 'together forever'! Oh, Ali. Can you believe it?"

"No," muttered Ali. But then again, maybe she could. Because wasn't it *just* like Sam to have something amazing like this happen to her? Ali looked at her twin and felt more different from her than she ever had before. She was so tired of seeing that dumb, happy smile, she wanted to shove Sam straight into the dirt.

But she didn't. "So, what do you mean tonight? Are you skipping the campfire?" she asked.

Sam shook her head. "No, of course I can't miss that. I'm going to go after. I'll wait till it's lights-out and everyone's asleep. I know it's totally crazy, but if you met him you'd understand. But, Ali"—she leaned in and whispered, even though no one else was around— "I'm only telling *you*, okay? It's a secret you have to keep. *Please*. We can consider this part of our deal, can't we?"

Ali nodded quickly, gently stroking her birthmark. "Oh, of course. Don't worry," she said. "I mean, why in the world would I ever want to tell?" She stretched out a smile, then she let it go. "But, you know, that doesn't mean that Gwen won't find out somehow."

"What do you mean?" asked Sam anxiously.

Ali shrugged. "Oh, I don't know. She might be up late with the other counselors since it's the last night for them, too. I thought I heard somewhere of this all-nighter tradition they have. But maybe whoever told me was totally wrong." She grinned and patted Sam's hand. "Forget it. You're right. She'll never know. Wow." She sighed. "Your very own dance in a moonlit clearing. I have to say, Sam, that sounds really, *really* romantic."

Neither Sam nor Ali said another word about Dennis for the whole rest of the day. They were much too busy, when they first got back, trying to become the other twin. As soon as they got to their cabin, they changed into each other's clothes. Then they worked on hiding Ali's birthmark. Of course, since neither twin had brought makeup to camp, they had to let the rest of their cabin in on their "little joke."

"This is really weird," said Jennifer as she dabbed at Ali's chin. It was Megan's makeup, but she did the honors since she was the most skilled of all of them.

"I think it's fun!" said Stefi. "Of course, you're not going to fool anyone, you know," she told the twins.

"Oh, I don't know." Jennifer paused to scratch a bugbite on her neck, then she blended in the final edge. She sat back to let the others see. "Check it out. What do you think?" she asked.

"Hey, not bad." Megan nodded.

"Let me see," Ali said.

Megan handed her a mirror, and she held it up to her face. She checked her chin from every angle. It looked as flawless as Sam's.

"Here, sit next to each other," said Stefi. She pulled Sam down onto the cot next to Ali so the bunkmates could study them, side by side.

Sam grinned. "So? Think we can do it?" she asked.

Stefi made a *who-knows* face.

"I say go for it," said Megan. "Isn't that the fun of being twins?"

Georgia raised a skeptical eyebrow. "I don't know. They look good now, but what happens when Ali opens her mouth?"

Ali replied by shooting her a sour, narrow-eyed smile. "I guess we're lucky then, aren't we, that the color war starts with silent lunch."

In fact, it *was* lucky for them. For being the only table that didn't talk at all, they earned an extra hundred points. Their team did well from there on too. As they had hoped, they swept the canoe races and got first in Frisbee golf. But they struggled in a few other competitions, such as archery, thanks to Sam (or Ali, as she called herself). By then her mind had wandered back to Dennis, and she could barely hit the target, let alone make a bull's-eye. Of course, since the real Ali never did either, no one seemed too surprised. They actually did fool a few people, including Gwen. Ali couldn't believe how nice Gwen was being to her—when she thought she was Sam. But they couldn't fool everyone forever. Georgia was almost right, but not exactly; people could tell Sam wasn't Ali as soon as *Sam* opened her mouth and said something sweet.

And then came the color war grand finale: the talent show.

"Okay, this has been fun," said Georgia, "but I think it's time to stop."

"What do you mean?" asked Sam and Ali together.

"This is the *talent* show," said Georgia. "And everyone knows who has the most talent, Sam. *You.* If we're going to win, we need you to be *you.*"

Sam bit her lip and glanced at Ali. Ali's face looked long and dark.

"Whoever agrees with me, raise your hand," said Georgia.

Unanimously the others lifted their arms.

"We're not saying you can't be in it," Jennifer told Ali.

"Of course not," the other girls said.

Ali looked at them all, then raised her own hand and bitterly rubbed her chin. The makeup smeared, revealing her birthmark. She wiped what came off on the side of her shorts.

"Whatever," she said. "I was getting bored of this anyway. I don't even want to be in the stupid talent show."

And with that she stormed away. Sam hurried to catch up.

"Wait, Ali!" she called. "Hang on. Please. Stop."

Ali turned.

"I tried," Sam began.

Ali rolled her eyes. "Yeah, I know."

"Will you . . ," Sam swallowed.

"Don't worry," Ali said. She looked over Sam's shoulder at their bunk. "I'm not going to tell Gwen about your little 'dance.' Do whatever you want. I don't care. Go show off your many talents. I'm sure Bunk 9 will win."

Bunk 9—and Team Red—did win, thanks to Sam's singing and a quick but impressive gymnastics routine. The girls tried to talk Ali into singing backup, but she refused.

"I'd rather roll around in poison ivy," Ali informed them.

She wished she could sit out the rest of the night and stay in the cabin all by herself, but Gwen had eventually noticed that Ali was missing from the festivities and told her that unless she was on her deathbed, she had to join everyone. So much for Gwen's being nice to her earlier that afternoon.

"You don't want to miss the awards!" she said.

Ali sighed. In fact, she did. She knew *she* wouldn't be getting any. She'd just be watching Sam.

The first round of awards went cabin by cabin. This was when the counselors recognized their campers' outstanding "accomplishments."

When Bunk 9's turn came, Gwen stood by the campfire. She pulled a pink bottle out of a bag.

"Our first award," she said, "goes to Jennifer Howard for Most Bugbites. Thanks for keeping the mosquitoes away from the rest of us, Jen!"

Jennifer jumped up and took it, grinning. "Thanks a lot. I just wish you'd given this to me four weeks ago," she said.

"Our next award goes to Georgia. Georgia, come on up here," Gwen said. She held up a lanyard from which dangled a toothbrush. She slipped it over Georgia's head. "For you, Georgia, the Lost and Found award, for losing your toothbrush twenty-six times this session. That's a record, I believe. So congrats!"

"This next award goes to our bunk's cutest couple, Stefi and Bingo," Gwen said to a chorus of giggles.

The How Does She Do It award went to Megan. It was a huge foil-covered question mark, which Gwen hung around her neck. "In recognition," Gwen explained, "of somehow going four whole weeks without doing your laundry."

"Let's see . . ." Gwen reached in her bag again and pulled out a toy watch. "Ah, Ali, would you come up here?"

Ali slowly obeyed. She stood by Gwen and let her buckle the toy around her wrist.

"The Sleepyhead award!" Gwen laughed—and so did the rest of the camp.

Ali muttered "Thanks" and slunk back out of the circle and sat as far back as she possibly could. There was just one more award for Gwen to give. She couldn't *wait* to see what it was for.

"And finally, for Sam." Gwen held up a gold star, which she pinned to Sam's chest. "The Neatest Bunk award!"

Sam bowed around the circle. "Thank you so much!"

From the shadows, Ali shrugged. *Wow, how boring,* she thought.

But that was only the beginning, it seemed. Gwen held up a ruler next. "And here's one more," she announced. "I don't always give this, but I had to for you, Sam." She pretended to knight Sam. "The Extra Mile award!"

That's more like it, Ali thought.

The more serious, official Camp Minnehaha awards came soon after, and Sam was on her feet through much of those. There were medals for Most Improved and Outstanding Spirit and for high points earned in various sports. Then came the highest award, given to one exceptional camper each summer. It was a small silver trophy called the Minnehaha Cup.

The director, Miss Abby, a tall woman with wiry, gray pigtails, stood up and spoke. Dried pink foam from a messy color war event called color tag still covered most of her camp shirt and cargo shorts. "I can't tell you what a hard decision this is for the staff to make," she said. "We are so proud of each and every one of you, and we hope each one of you is just as proud of yourself." But this year, she explained, the vote had been almost unanimous. "Samantha Harmon," she declared, "it is with great pleasure that I present to you the Minnehaha Cup!"

The air was instantly filled with snaps and whoops, Camp Minnehaha's official form of applause. Stunned, Sam rose to her feet and walked toward Miss Abby. She caught a glimpse of Gwen, who was standing, and saw her wink and let out an extra-loud "whoop!" The rest of Bunk 9 had jumped up and were cheering at the tops of their lungs too. Only Ali stayed silent and seated. She was thinking again of how it must feel to be Sam. She'd hoped that spending the day switching places might give her a clue. But it didn't. Instead it ended up making Ali feel more different than ever from her.

Sam stood by the fire, meanwhile, just trying to take it all in. The Minnehaha Cup! She never thought she'd earn it. Well, she'd hoped, but she'd been sure she'd lost any chance as soon as Gwen caught her sneaking off. But no. Gwen must have really had a lot of faith in her, as well as Miss Abby and everyone else.

"Thank you," Sam said as she took the cup with a humble little bow. She looked at it and saw her face in the polished surface, smiling back at her. It was a face that had spent the whole day thinking way more about a boy than camp. *What would Gwen and Miss Abby think,* she wondered, *if they found out about that?*

Head down, she walked back to her place in the circle and rejoined her proud bunkmates. They jumped up to hug her as the whole camp stood and linked arms. It was time to sing, for the last time that summer, the Minnehaha song.

> *Oh, Friends of Minnehaha,*
> *Together we will stay;*
> *In fair or stormy weather,*
> *Friends forever and a day.*

A sharp pang of guilt lodged in Sam's throat and made her voice shaky and hoarse. Tears welled in her eyes as she thought, *I love this place so much!* At the same time she thought about Dennis and smiled. She could feel the sparks even then from his touch. *But is he worth it?* she suddenly wondered. After all, he *was* just a boy.

Oh, what am I thinking? she suddenly told herself. He wasn't "just a boy" at all!

From the first moment they'd met (so awkwardly!) she'd sensed he was different from everyone else. And he wouldn't just be a summer boyfriend, no matter how far away he lived. They would find a way to be "together forever." She knew that deep down in her soul. She just wished she didn't have to sneak away to see him. A moonlit dance was wonderful to think about, but the risks were so great. She wasn't even nervous, she suddenly realized, about hiking through the woods at night alone. But she was deathly afraid of being caught. Was she brave enough to go?

CHAPTER 13

The answer came that night, long after lights-out, when the last girls who had sworn to stay up all night finally gave in and closed their eyes.

Then the door of Bunk 9 slowly opened, and a girl in a hooded sweatshirt tiptoed out. Carefully she made her way past the cabins, the main lodge, and the sports fields, until she came to the Old Stump Trail. Then at last she turned on the flashlight she'd been holding tightly in her hand. The beam it gave off was weak from four weeks of late-night trips to the latrine, but it was still enough to help her find the path through the tall, whispering trees.

Suddenly, two lights flashed just ahead of her. She stopped, afraid to move.

"Me-ew."

She smiled. "Hey, Magic," she whispered, bending down and holding out her hand. The cat was basically invisible—like ink spilled on a road. He padded over silently and ran his back under her palm, then he moved along and disappeared into the night.

The girl kept moving too. *If only the moon would come out,* she thought. Where was it anyway? Hadn't the boy in the clearing promised the moon would be *full* for their dance? She paused to peer up through the branches and realized she couldn't see a single star. The sky was a thick black blanket propped up by leafy arms. She held her flashlight close to her body and tiptoed on, as if she were afraid of waking the forest up.

With each step her heart beat a little faster. She was eager but nervous, too, and not just because she was in the woods in the middle of the night all alone. She also knew what she was doing was wrong, to some people at least. And she knew how bad it would be if she were to get caught. But there were some times, she'd decided, when you just had to follow your gut. You couldn't sit and worry about what was "right" or "wrong."

"Who-whoo!"

She jumped at a sudden sound behind her, and her light swung wildly as she turned. She waved the beam like a sword down the trail behind her, trying to see what was back there. It definitely wasn't Magic. She tensed. Every tree looked like a monster—or something that one could hide behind.

Suddenly two more bright dots flashed at her. "Ah!" she gasped. They disappeared as the light swept by.

Were they eyes? She tried to find them again.

"Who-*whoo!*"

She caught the face of a large, solemn owl on a branch and let out a heavy sigh.

She watched him blink one eye, then the other, before his head turned completely around. She gasped, then suddenly realized she was looking at his back. She lowered her flashlight and let him melt back into the night. Hopefully, that would be the last living thing— except for Dennis Shaw, of course—that she met on her hike that night.

Finally she came to the place she'd been looking out for, where the wide Old Stump Trail curved, and a smaller, much less-traveled one split off and went straight. She took a deep breath and ducked under a branch and carefully pushed her way in through the dense undergrowth.

Now she really wished she had the moon to help her. With nothing but the misty beam from her flashlight, she could barely tell where to place her footsteps. She kept her head down and looked for signs that someone had recently been through. A few broken twigs and a familiar footprint made her feel a little more secure. With almost every step forward, though, a rogue root or vine seemed to send her stumbling back two. Branches swatted at her from the right and the left, and she pulled the sweatshirt down around her head as far as she possibly could. The smell was strong—but she was grateful for its deep, heavy hood.

She wondered how much farther away the clearing was. She had to be getting pretty close by now. She tried to guess how long she'd been walking and what time it might be. . . .

Oh no! she thought all of a sudden. *What if I get there too late?*

What if Dennis gets tired of waiting for me and goes back to camp?

Or what if, the thought suddenly hit her, *he doesn't even* come? What if he gets sick—or just stays home—like he did before?

What if this whole late-night mission was for nothing at all? What if she was stuck out here alone, waiting all night in the dark woods?

She couldn't bear to think about it, and yet the thought festered in her mind. She didn't even notice, in fact, when the trail abruptly stopped. The next thing she knew, the trees were gone and there was soft grass beneath her shoes.

She was in the clearing. She had made it. Eagerly she looked around. Her flashlight beam was frail by this time. Her batteries had just about reached the end of their lives. But it didn't matter, she realized happily as she spotted Dennis Shaw. Even in the darkness the clearing seemed to glow, and Dennis gave off his own supernatural light. His hair shone almost silver, and so did his eyes. They locked on her like lasers as he reached out a hand. She could feel herself moving toward him before the idea even came to her mind. All she could think at the moment was, *I did it! I'm really here!*

It was a night she knew she'd never forget, no matter how long she lived.

As she got closer, she could see he had a big bouquet of blue flowers, which he held out to her. And then, as if he couldn't wait a second longer, he ran up and took her hand. She felt a shock and looked down, surprised not to see any actual sparks shoot out.

"You came! I knew you would! I'm so glad!" His face could hardly contain his smile. "Now we can be together forever, at last!" he exclaimed.

He offered her the flowers, and she took them happily, letting her flashlight fall to the ground. She buried her nose in the silky petals and drank in their sweet smell. *It's such a nice change from the mossy musk of the forest,* she thought, *but a bit overpowering, as well.* While she raised her head and tried to clear it, he took her hand in both of his.

"Thank you for coming!" he said. "You don't know how lonely I've been here all these years by myself."

Dreamily she nodded. Then suddenly, beneath her hood, she cocked her head.

Wait, she thought. *What did he mean by 'all these years'?*

"I . . . I thought you were from Camp Hiawatha?" she said.

Still grinning, he nodded. "Oh, I am." Then a corner

of his lip turned down. "Or really, I *was*. Ten years ago."

"Ten years?" Her mouth felt dry. Her throat grew tight. Her spine went stiff with dread.

Slowly he nodded. "I've been stuck here ever since." He moved his head around to indicate the clearing, but his eyes stayed firmly fixed on her. "This clearing, it's enchanted—or depending on how you look at it, I guess, cursed. I actually came across it accidentally one night when I snuck away from camp. It wasn't my first time sneaking out." He laughed. "But it was the first time I'd gone through *here*. I'd heard about it, of course," he said. "There was a rumor at Hiawatha that it was haunted, but I didn't care. I just wanted to get away. And I knew it was the fastest way to your camp, Minnehaha, where I hoped to meet up with this girl. Nobody special, of course." He grinned. "I met her at a dance. But you're a lot prettier," he said. "It was this same time of year, late August, and it was a full moon too. But almost as soon as I got to this clearing, a lightning storm came up out of the blue, and I went into that cabin thinking I'd wait it out." He paused. "I should have kept going, but it was probably already too late."

"What happened?" she whispered, afraid of the

answer—but at the same time she had to know.

"I'm not really sure," he said. "All I know is the storm passed and the moon came back out, and suddenly the whole place was glowing—and I was too."

Clearly, he could feel her trying to pull her hand back. He squeezed more tightly in response. "Don't worry, it didn't *hurt*," he assured her. "It's more like you're on vibrate—until it's all done. I didn't know what was happening then, but now I do, I guess. Everything here—everything around you, including me, is under a spell. Most of the time I'm not even here, in fact. I'm in a place where time stands still. But for a few days a year—the full moon in August—I materialize again. But I can't escape. I'm trapped within the bounds of this clearing. And you can't imagine how lonely it is."

His smile was gone now, replaced by a deadly serious stare. "But then I saw you through the trees while you were out hiking the other day, and, I don't know, something just clicked. I could actually imagine spending eternity like this—if you were here to share it with. I could tell, you know, how much everyone liked you and how much fun you were to be with. Not like that other girl. Is she your sister? The one who kept kicking mushrooms and tossing rocks?" He leaned in closer. "That's why I sent you that dream the other night."

She was shaking her head by now, tugging at her hand still clasped in his.

"Yes!" He nodded. "It came from me! I hoped it would work and bring you here, and it did, perfectly! Did you also know," he went on, "that I sent nightmares to the other girls? It wasn't just to keep them away, either. It was fun, too, I have to admit."

She had a feeling his smile had returned, but she couldn't be sure. By now her flashlight had died completely. The clearing was as dark as the sky. All she could see were the gleaming silver circles of light that were his eyes.

The things he was saying were impossible! And yet she knew in her heart they were true. She also knew she had to get away from Dennis Shaw and the clearing as fast as she could.

"No!" She tried to pull away harder. "This is a mistake. Please! Let me go."

"Mistake?" He laughed. "Oh no. I don't think so," he said. His grip on her hand grew even tighter, until she was sure her bones would break. "What's wrong,

Sam? I don't understand." His voice had a sudden sharp and wounded edge. "You seemed to like me just this afternoon. Remember? I *asked* you if you wanted to be together forever, and you told me that you did. Now you want to take that back? I know this is all a big shock, but you'll get used to it eventually. Trust me. I did."

"But—"

The girl froze then as an icy wind whipped across them both. It carried a scent, pungent and sour, which stung her nose and stole her breath. At the same time, green mist seemed to roll into the clearing.

She gazed up, and so did Dennis, to watch the clouds roll apart. The moon emerged so full and bright that she had to shield her eyes. In the distance she could see streaks of lightning cracking against the sky.

"I'm sorry." Dennis shook his head. "There are no buts anymore. The spell is cast, I'm afraid." His smile by now was even brighter than the silver orb above. "But we're together *forever* now, Sam. Just like you wanted. Isn't it great?"

And with that, he let go of her hand and gently pulled back her hood.

CHAPTER 14

The next morning, Jennifer Howard woke up and pulled the sheet over her head. It was the last day of camp, and she just wasn't ready to get up and start it yet.

She wondered what time it was. Maybe seven? The sun was already inching in through the window, but it still seemed quiet outside. Of course, the whole camp had been up so late last night, it was sure to be a slow morning for everyone.

The crumpled sheet drifted back down to her shoulders as she stretched and rolled onto her side. She could see good old Sam's bunk, already empty and neatly made. But she knew for a fact that Sam's bunk wasn't much of a wake-up gauge. Sam was always the first one up and out of bed after all. By now she was probably saying good-bye to the chickens, or picking berries for Kay.

Then her eyes moved to Ali's bed, and what she saw surprised her so much that she bolted up and banged her head.

"Ouch!" she cried, rubbing her part and finding a brand new mosquito bite right there.

"What? What's wrong?" She heard Megan call down. "Why are you yelling? Go back to sleep."

"Sorry," Jennifer said. "But I think it's kind of late."

"It can't be," Megan groaned. She leaned over the edge and peered at Jennifer through tousled hair and sleepy eyes.

"Oh yeah?" Jennifer nodded over toward Ali's rumpled bunk. "Check it out."

The bed was empty.

"No way!" Megan gasped. She looked around at the other bunks, which were all still occupied. "Hey, Georgia! Stefi! Get up!" she called. "Ali's gone. We overslept!"

"No, you didn't." It was Sam, walking into the room. She looked worried.

"No? Then where's Ali?" Jennifer asked her.

Sam held out her hands. "I don't know. I thought

maybe I'd see her in the latrine, but she wasn't there or anywhere else."

She looked around for some kind of clue as to where her sister might be. Sam couldn't remember the last time that she'd slept later than Ali. And then, purely by accident, her eyes fell on the hook on the end of her bed . . . the hook where she'd hung Dennis Shaw's sweatshirt . . .

The hook that now was bare.

And there, on the floor beneath it, sat Megan's makeup jar.

Instantly, Sam realized exactly where Ali must have gone.

Seconds later, it seemed, the whole bunk was dressed and flying down the Old Stump Trail. They didn't exactly understand Sam's explanation. (A boy? A dance? In the moonlight?) But they knew something must be very wrong if Ali had gone into the woods alone at night and hadn't returned to camp yet.

They came to the point where the trail to the clearing started, and as soon as Sam took it, the other girls exchanged uneasy looks. They remembered the nightmare that all of them had shared. Suddenly their search took a whole new and much more frightening turn.

"Do you see any sign of her?" asked Sam.

But no, nobody did.

"Ali!" they all cried. "Ali! Can you hear us? Are you there?"

But there was no sound except for the echo that their anxious voices left in the air.

When they finally reached the clearing, each girl expected to find a scene straight out of her dream: glowing green and eerie—or impossibly lovely, in Sam's case. But what they found instead was a ragged circle of thin, tired grass. There were no flowers or dainty butterflies, just a few old anthills with no ants. There was, however, a cabin -but it, too, was rather plain. It simply had four log walls, a thinning shingle roof, two dirty windows and a door. They could see from where they stood that it was wide open, and their hearts filled with hope that Ali was inside.

"Ali!"

They ran up to the cabin together. Sam was the first one in.

"Do you see her?" Jennifer asked, slipping in behind her.

Sam peered in every dark corner. "No," she softly replied.

There was no Ali. And no Dennis.

No life, in fact, of any kind.

"Wait. Here's something," said Jennifer suddenly.

"What?" Sam turned to her.

She stood in the doorway with a thick red bundle that she'd picked up off the floor. Gingerly Jennifer unfolded it and let it dangle from her hands. The words CAMP HIAWATHA were easy to make out. And yet they looked so faded, and the fabric looked so worn, as if the thing had lain there moldering for ten years, or even more.

It can't be Dennis's, thought Sam. And yet something told her that it was.

It was the same numb, haunted feeling that told her that her sister was gone . . . forever?

CHAPTER 1

Click.

Ashley blinked in the sudden brightness. The bare lightbulb overhead swung from a rusty chain, casting shadows all over her new bedroom. She squinted in the harsh light, but it was the best she could do until she unpacked the little purple lamp that had sat on her bedside table for as long as she could remember.

Besides, she told herself, glancing from the boxes scattered over the pocked floor to the four-foot crack running down the wall, *it's not like this room could look any worse.*

Ashley sighed, for the thousandth time, as she remembered her old bedroom back in Atlanta. It was perfect in every way, from the pale aqua paint on the walls to the window seat that overlooked the alley, a quiet place in a bustling city. But that was all gone now; Ashley knew she'd probably never see her room again. Maybe, right this very minute, somebody else was sitting in her old room, starting to unpack a bunch of boxes.

Lucky, Ashley thought, flopping back on her bare mattress and staring at the stain-spotted ceiling. She knew she should put the sheets on her bed, but she just didn't feel like doing anything.

There was a knock at the door. Ashley could tell from the four strong raps that it was her mother. *Maybe if I ignore her, she'll go away,* Ashley thought.

The knock came again, and then the door creaked open.

"Hey, Pumpkin!" Mrs. McDowell called out in a cheerful voice. "How's it going in here? Want some help?"

Ashley shrugged and rolled over on the bed so that she was facing the window. It was getting dark outside—a deeper darkness than she was used to. It never felt dark in Atlanta, not really dark, not with all the streetlights and headlights and towering buildings whose windows glowed all night long. But this far out in the country, light was harder to come by once the sun went down.

The bed creaked as Mrs. McDowell sat behind Ashley and started rubbing her back. Ashley inched away. She knew she was probably hurting her mom's feelings, but it was hard to care. After all, it wasn't like her mom and dad had cared about *her* feelings when they'd decided to sell their apartment and buy this rundown farm out in the middle of nowhere.

"This is going to be a really great thing, Ashley," Mrs. McDowell said yet again. "Just try to have faith, okay? I know change is hard and stressful and scary—"

"Scary? Um, no. I'm not *scared*. I'm *bored*. I hate it here."

"You hate it here?" Mrs. McDowell said. "Pumpkin, we've only been in Heaton Corners for, oh, five hours or so. All I ask is that you give it a chance. You know Dad and I wouldn't make a decision this big if we didn't think it was the best thing for everyone."

"But you didn't even *ask* me," Ashley replied, blinking back tears. "I don't *want* to live on a smelly farm, Mom. I miss Atlanta so much."

Mrs. McDowell sighed. "We really regret not leaving the city before Maya went to college," she said in a quiet voice. "We don't want to make the same mistake with you. Maya spent her whole childhood cooped up in that apartment—"

"Yeah, and she loved it!" Ashley interrupted. "And so did I!"

"Can you try to think of it as an adventure?" Mrs. McDowell asked, and there was something so vulnerable in her voice that Ashley finally sat up and looked at her. "You know there's something really exciting about a fresh start, going to a whole new school and meeting all kinds of new people! And we'll have the homestead up and running before you know it—the chicks will arrive in a few days; won't that be fun? Little fluffy baby chickens? And next spring we'll get a cow!"

Ashley started to laugh. It was such a ridiculous thing to say—"we'll get a cow!"—that she couldn't help herself. And she couldn't miss the relief that flooded her mom's eyes.

"And maybe," Ashley said, wishing that she wasn't giving in so easily but saying it anyway, "we can fix that horrible crack over there? It looks like the wall got struck by lightning."

Mrs. McDowell smiled as she patted Ashley's knee. "Of course. I'll have Dad come take a look—we can probably patch that crack by the end of the week. And then we'll get the walls primed for painting. Have you thought about what color you want? Maybe a nice, sunny yellow?"

"Aqua," Ashley said firmly. "Just like my old room."

"All right," Mrs. McDowell said. "Whatever you want. Listen, Dad went to get pizza; I think he'll be back in an hour or so."

"That long?" Ashley asked. "To grab pizza?"

"Well, it turns out there's no pizza place in Heaton Corners," Mrs. McDowell said, sighing. "So he had to drive all the way to Walthrop."

Ashley sneered. "Seriously. What kind of town doesn't have a pizza place? Heaton Corners is the worst. The worst."

"No, no, it's not so bad," Mrs. McDowell said. "We'll learn to make our own pizza! And after we get the vegetable garden going next summer, we'll even make our own sauce! With our own tomatoes!"

Yeah. Great, Ashley thought. *Or, you know, we could get a pizza from Bernini's in, like, ten minutes. If we still lived in Atlanta.*

"So, come down when you can and help me find the plates," Mrs. McDowell said as she stood up. On her way out, she paused by the door. "Oh, Ashley? Did I see your bike out back?"

"Yeah, probably."

"Go out and put it in the barn, okay?"

"Why?" Ashley argued. "We're in the middle of nowhere, remember? Nobody's going to steal it."

"Probably not," Mrs. McDowell replied. Then she pointed at the window. "But it looks like it's going to rain tonight. You see those thunderheads gathering? So go ahead and get your bike in the barn so it doesn't rust. Thanks, Pumpkin."

Ashley sighed heavily as her mom left. Then she halfheartedly started rummaging through one of the boxes on the floor. She didn't exactly feel like unpacking, but she definitely didn't feel like rushing outside to put away her bike just because her mom said so.

Of course, there was no way for Ashley to know that that particular carton held her Memory Box, a dark-purple shoebox that was crammed with photos, cards, and funny notes from her best friends in Atlanta. Just seeing Nora and Lucy's handwriting made Ashley feel homesick. By the time she'd finished rereading every single note, it was pitch-black outside.

And her mom was shouting from the kitchen.

"Ashley! Your bike! And I'm going to need your help in here!"

Ashley shoved the Memory Box under her bed and went downstairs, walking right past the kitchen without saying a word to her mom. Her flip-flops were near the back door, where she'd kicked them off after the movers had left. One look out the window told Ashley that she would need a flashlight to find the barn. Luckily, there was a flashlight hanging right next to the door. Ashley guessed that the last people who'd lived here had found themselves in the same situation.

She switched on the flashlight and stepped outside. Its bright-yellow beam arced through the night sky, then quickly faded to a dull orange. Ashley shook the flashlight and smacked it against her palm until it glowed a little brighter.

Typical, she thought. *I bet the batteries will die as soon as I get into the barn.*

The thought made Ashley walk a little faster as she wheeled her bike through the overgrown goldenrod toward the barn. It hadn't started raining yet, but the weeds were damp with evening dew, and she shivered as they slapped against her bare legs. And her toes were *freezing.* Ashley hated to admit it, but her mom was right: Sandal season was *definitely* coming to an end.

As Ashley walked, she remembered what her mom had said about Maya: "We really regret not leaving the city before Maya went to college." *It just shows how clueless my parents are,* Ashley thought. Her big sister had *never* wanted to live in the country. That's why she'd decided to go to college in Chicago. It had been a little over a month since Maya had moved into her dorm, and Ashley missed her every day. Talking on the phone or chatting online just wasn't the same. And Chicago felt so far away to Ashley. It wasn't even in the same state. It wasn't even in the same time zone!

Just before Ashley reached the barn, the flashlight died, but in a stroke of luck the clouds parted for a moment, letting through enough moonlight that she could lift the heavy iron latch on the barn door. The only sound Ashley could hear was the soft *squeeeeeeak* of the bike's gears as she pushed it into the barn.

The air in the barn was dry and dusty; it smelled of caked dirt and hay. The moment Ashley stepped in from the barn door, it slammed shut with such a loud bang that she jumped. Without even the weak beam of the flashlight to guide her steps, Ashley was plunged into pitch-black darkness. She stretched her arm out as far as it would reach, until her fingers grazed the rough, unfinished wood of the barn wall. Then she took one careful step at a time until she found a spot to leave her bike. Ashley leaned it against the wall and turned to leave.

C-r-r-r-r-unch.

She froze.

What, Ashley thought as her heart started to pound, *did I just step on?*

There was something leathery—something papery— something scaly—something she couldn't quite place flicking against her bare skin. Was it slithering over her feet, twining around her ankles? Or was that just her imagination?

Had it been *waiting* for someone to set foot inside this old, abandoned barn?

Stop it, Ashley told herself firmly. She was a city girl. She was not the kind of person who freaked out over every little thing. With a surge of confidence, she hit the flashlight against her palm again.

Thwak. Thwak. Thwak.

Suddenly a pale beam flashed across the barn. The flashlight was working again, for a minute, at least.

Ashley pointed the flashlight at her feet. It took a moment—longer, probably—for her to realize what she was standing in; some part of her brain couldn't, *wouldn't* accept it. There were so many that she couldn't count them, especially because of the way they wriggled—

Wait. *Were* they moving? Or was that just the effect of her clumsy feet as she stumbled, trying to escape?

Either way, Ashley didn't stick around to find out. She screamed—she couldn't help it—as the weak light from the flashlight died again. Ashley rushed out of the barn, still screaming, and her screams echoed across the farm, almost as if they were ricocheting off the heavy clouds that were crowding the sky once more.

She was so preoccupied by the memory of those slithery *things* on her feet, and so distracted by the utter darkness, that she didn't see the tall figure step out from the shadows . . .

Until a pair of strong hands grabbed her shoulders and held on tight!

CHAPTER 2

Ashley screamed so loudly that her whole body shuddered from the effort. She twisted away violently, flailing her arms, until she recognized the voice of the person holding her.

"Ashley! Ashley! Stop, Ashley, what's wrong?"

"Dad!" she cried. An overwhelming feeling of relief flooded through her veins, but it was soon replaced by embarrassment. "When did you—"

"I just got back from Walthrop," Mr. McDowell replied. He pointed at the pizza box he had dropped on the ground. "Ashley, what happened? I got out of the truck and heard you screaming—"

"Oh," Ashley said. "I was, um, in the barn and

I stepped in, I don't know, like, a nest of—*snakes* or something."

"A nest of snakes?" Mr. McDowell repeated. "What kind?"

"I don't know," Ashley replied, staring at the ground. "I didn't exactly stick around to find out. And, besides, the flashlight went dead."

"I want to take a look at that nest," Mr. McDowell said. He switched on the super-bright LCD penlight on his key chain. "Want to come with me?"

"That's okay," Ashley said at once. "I think I've spent enough time in the barn tonight. Thanks anyway."

Mr. McDowell stooped down to pick up the pizza box. "Would you take the pizza inside?" he said. "I'll be back in a minute."

Ashley watched her dad's silhouette move away into the darkness. "Dad, wait," she said, panic creeping into her voice. "Just—just leave it. You can go look at the snakes tomorrow, okay? Please?"

She heard him chuckle in the darkness. "I'll be careful," he told her.

Ashley didn't reply as she walked up to the house. She didn't see the point of poking around in the barn when it was pitch-black outside.

"Oh, is that the pizza?" Mrs. McDowell asked as Ashley walked into the kitchen. "Finally! I'm starving! Where's your dad?"

"In the barn," Ashley said.

"The barn?" Mrs. McDowell sounded puzzled. "Why? It's time to eat."

Ashley shrugged. She didn't feel like getting into it. "Here. This flashlight needs new batteries."

"Okay. Just put it on the counter and I'll find some later."

Ashley set the flashlight next to the pizza box and peeked inside it. She had to admit that the pizza, smothered in vegetables and crisp pepperoni, looked pretty good—so good that she broke off a piece of the crust and started nibbling it. Then she made a face. "It's kind of cold," she pointed out.

"Ashley, you know I hate it when you start eating right out of the box," Mrs. McDowell sighed. "You'll have to microwave your piece if it bothers you."

Ugh, rubbery pizza, Ashley thought. But she didn't say anything, because at that moment her dad walked through the back door.

"I found your snake pit, Ashley," he said as he casually tossed something at her feet.

Ashley jumped back and shrieked before she could stop herself.

"What is *that*?" Mrs. McDowell asked with disgust dripping from her voice. "And why is it in my house?"

"It's a snake skin," Mr. McDowell explained. "I thought Ash'd be relieved to know that she only stumbled through a pile of snake *skins*—not real snakes."

Ashley shuddered. "Ugh, gross," she said defensively. "And it was dark and I felt them, like, flicking against my bare feet! How was I supposed to know they weren't alive?"

Ashley's parents exchanged a smile, and she rolled her eyes. She wished they would start treating her like an adult—instead of some little pet who made them laugh.

"Honey, we're living on a farm now," Mrs. McDowell reminded Ashley—as if she could forget. "If you're going outside, you need to wear your boots—or at least your sneakers."

"Especially when you go to the barn," Mr. McDowell added. "Nobody's lived here for at least five years. There could be rusty nails, brown recluse spiders—"

"Okay, okay, I get it," Ashley cut him off. "Can we please eat now?"

"Yes. Just as soon as your dad takes that thing outside," Mrs. McDowell said firmly.

"Weird, though, isn't it?" Mr. McDowell said as he picked up the snake skin. "Snakes don't molt in a nest. So this pile must've been collected by somebody. And it must've taken a long time to find so many snake skins."

Mrs. McDowell waved her hand dismissively and took the pizza box out to the dining room table. "Time to stop talking about snakes and start eating. Don't forget to wash your hands before you come to the table, you two."

As Ashley washed her hands at the deep, stained sink in the kitchen, she glanced out the window. She could see a few fallen leaves swoop by on a gust of wind, and she wished—for the thousandth time—that they could move back to the city.

WANT MORE CREEPINESS?

Then you're in luck, because P. J. Night has some more scares for you and your friends!

A Message from Ali

Ali Harmon has a message for you. Unscramble each of these words from the story and write the circled letters in order on the blanks on the next page.

KNBU ◯ _ _ _

MINEHHANA _ _ _ _ ◯ _ _ _ _

AATHAHWI _ _ _ ◯ _ _ _ _

AINRTLE _ ◯ _ _ _ _ _

EJIFERNN _ _ _ _ _ _ _ ◯

NEGW _ _ ◯ _

UPSMT _ ◯ _ _ _

OAHNRM ◯ _ _ _ _ _

FEITS _ _ ◯ _ _

EMNAG _ _ _ _ ⦾

LAI _ _ ⦾

CIGMA _ _ _ ⦾ _ _

TTHAWSSREI _ _ _ _ _ _ ⦾ _ _ _

ITALR ⦾ _ _ _ _ _

MSA _ _ ⦾

AYK _ ⦾ _

RUOCLONSE _ _ _ _ _ _ _ _ ⦾

CNAED _ _ _ _ ⦾

Write the boxed letters in order. What is Ali's
message?

_ _ _ _ _ _ _   _ _ _

_ _ _ _ _ _ _ _ _ _ !

YOU'RE INVITED TO ...
CREATE YOUR OWN SCARY STORY!

Do you want to turn your sleepover into a creepover? Telling a spooky story is a great way to set the mood. P. J. Night has written a few sentences to get you started. Fill in the rest of the story and have fun scaring your friends.

You can also collaborate with your friends on this story by taking turns. Have everyone at your sleepover sit in a circle. Pick one person to start. She will add a sentence or two to the story, cover what she wrote with a piece of paper, leaving only the last word or phrase visible, and then pass the story to the next girl. Once everyone has taken a turn, read the scary story you created together aloud!

Camp _____ is like no other sleepaway camp in the world. When you pull up to the front gate, a dilapidated sign hangs from a pole. The pool is filled with green water, and the counselors only know how to frown. But the worst part of Camp _____ is at night, when you turn out the lights, and come face to face with . . .

_____

_____

_____

_____

_____

_____

_____

_____

_____

_____

_____

_____

THE END

A lifelong night owl, **P. J. NIGHT** often works furiously into the wee hours of the morning, writing down spooky tales and dreaming up new stories of the supernatural and otherworldly. Although P. J.'s whereabouts are unknown at this time, we suspect the author lives in a drafty, old mansion where the floorboards creak when no one is there and the flickering candlelight creates shadows that creep along the walls. We truly wish we could tell you more, but we've been sworn to keep P. J.'s identity a secret . . . and it's a secret we will take to our graves!

What's better than reading a really spooky story?

Writing your own!

You just read a great book. It gave you ideas, didn't it? Ideas for your next story: characters...plot...setting... You can't wait to grab a notebook and a pen and start writing it all down.

It happens a lot. *Ideas just pop into your head.* In between classes entire story lines take shape in your imagination. And when you start writing, the words flow, and you end up with notebooks crammed with your creativity.

It's okay, you aren't alone. Come to **KidPub**, the web's largest gathering of kids just like you. Share your stories with thousands of people from all over the world. Meet new friends and see what they're writing. Test your skills in one of our writing contests. See what other kids think about your stories.

And above all, *come to write!*

www.KidPub.com